RUBY'S WAR

Frank Ruby, a former Confederate soldier, arrives in the Yankee town of Watts Ridge and experiences bigotry and hatred. Next day, Jed Hanson, whose wife had been murdered by rebels, trails him. The planned bushwhack fails and Ruby shows the man mercy. Yancey Clark, a Confederate soldier, had led the raiders who murdered Martha Hanson. Clark continues to raid and plunder and Ruby is in danger as he struggles for justice. It can only end in a bloody confrontation on the streets of Watts Ridge.

Books by Skeeter Dodds
in the Linford Western Library:

RIKER'S GOLD

SKEETER DODDS

RUBY'S WAR

Complete and Unabridged

LINFORD
Leicester

First published in Great Britain in 2004 by
Robert Hale Limited
London

First Linford Edition
published 2006
by arrangement with
Robert Hale Limited
London

British Library CIP Data

Dodds, Skeeter
  Ruby's war.—Large print ed.—
Linford western library
1. Western stories
2. Large type books
I. Title
823.9′2 [F]

ISBN 1–84617–167–9

Published by
F. A. Thorpe (Publishing)
Anstey, Leicestershire

Set by Words & Graphics Ltd.
Anstey, Leicestershire
Printed and bound in Great Britain by
T. J. International Ltd., Padstow, Cornwall

This book is printed on acid-free paper

1

'Rebs ain't welcome in Watts Ridge, mister!'

Frank Ruby ignored the large-bellied man who had been sitting on a rocker on the saloon porch when he had ridden up, but who was now towering over him while he secured his horse to the saloon hitch rail.

'Hey, fellas,' he said to men joining him, 'my eyesight ain't too good these days. Is that tunic grey or' — he laid heavy emphasis on the next word out of his mouth — '*yella*?'

His cronies, layabouts and liquor-bummers, left their chairs and formed a circle round large-belly, closing the circle as the man continued with his challenge to Ruby.

'The town's got two ends, Reb,' he growled. 'The way you came in' — he pointed to the opposite end of Main

— 'and the way you'll be leaving.'

'Yeah. You tell him, Charlie,' a crony barked.

Passers-by were stopping, gathering in small whispering groups, none keen to be seen as an associate of Ruby's tormentor but all obviously wanting what he wanted by proxy. Ruby could understand the town's anger at seeing a Reb tunic, the wounds of war were still raw, but the fact was that having lost everything, his wardrobe was limited to the clothes he stood up in. Having been at a crossroads between opposing forces in the final bitter and bloody months of the conflict, Watts Ridge had suffered more than its fair share of death and destruction, a lot of it caused by the swiftly moving Yankee advance. But as in all conflicts, judgements were clouded and perceptions warped. It was the lot of the vanquished to be blamed for every atrocity, and the bounty of the victorious to get all the credit.

Shame was the lot of both Reb and Yankee, because American had killed

American; brother had butchered brother; neighbour had slain neighbour. Houses were divided. Territories torn asunder. And the legacy of bitterness would make for years of hostility, not on the grand scale of war, but in the close confines of towns and hamlets, mud cabins and great halls.

Towns like Watts Ridge.

That was the horror of all civil wars. But those who had chosen to wear the grey of the South would spend many years being pariahs. Frank Ruby fully understood that had the South been victorious and were he in Kentucky or Lousiana there would be men just like the man challenging him now, saying the same thing.

We don't want you in our Reb town, Yankee.

'I'm just passing through,' Ruby said. 'I'm not looking for trouble. Just stopped to slake my thirst.'

He went to enter the saloon, but the circle of men closed round him blocking his path. He repeated, emphatically, 'Like I said. I'm not looking for trouble.'

The man called Charlie hitched up his trousers and dropped balled fists to his side. 'You don't hear too good, d'ya, Reb?' he bellowed.

'I hear fine, mister,' Frank said, quietly; a quietness which Charlie obviously interpreted as timidity or fear. And like all bullies, Ruby's apparent reticence to fight his corner fuelled Charlie's belligerence.

'I'm going to teach you a lesson, you stinkin' Reb.' He started down the saloon steps, confident that in a couple of minutes from now his victim would be lying bleeding and battered in the street, if not dead.

The circle formed a fighting ring.

In his quiet way, Ruby warned the man. 'I wouldn't try what you have in mind, mister. You'll only come out worse for wear.'

Charlie, who had at least twenty pounds advantage over Ruby, opened his eyes wide as if he had seen a ghost.

He shivered, and mocked, 'Jeez, Reb. I'm real scared.'

'You should be,' Frank Ruby said, deadpan.

'Ya know,' the large-bellied trouble-stirrer growled, 'I've had 'bout enough of you, Reb.' He sniffed the air. 'You're makin' the air in this town smell real bad.'

A fist which seemed the size of a boulder swung at Ruby and almost caught him unawares. Like a lot of big men, Charlie had a swiftness of fist and foot out of kilter with his bulk. Ruby danced away, but was lucky not to have been pole-axed. Charlie paced him, only a hair's-breadth of space separating them, his fists swiping the air. Ruby knew that even a glancing blow from the boulder-sized fists would send him ass over head halfway across the territory. Slugging it out was not an option. He would have to be patient and wait for an opportunity to duck inside or under Charlie's maulers when, riled enough by the ineffectiveness of his lumbering lunges he would stretch an inch too far, leaving a gap through which Ruby could hopefully nip in to land a blow that would at least slow up the ape-like giant.

'Break his back, Charlie!' a bow-legged runt urged.

'Yeah, Charlie,' another pitched in. 'See how cocky the bastard is when he's in a cripple's chair.'

Ruby, though fleet of foot, was hard put to match Charlie's weaving foot-work. He reckoned that what he was facing in large-belly, was a bare-knuckled pugilist gone to seed — but not as much as Ruby was beginning to wish he had.

A sledge-hammer blow connected with Ruby's left shoulder and spun him like a top. He crashed against the saloon hitch rail. His back arched with the force of the blow. Had he been less fit and hard-muscled as he was, his spine would have snapped like a dry twig.

Swiftly closing in, sensing a quick

victory, Charlie planted his boot on Frank Ruby's foot, applying the pressure of every ounce of his weight. A million needles of pain shot up Ruby's leg into his lower back. The boot anchored him for the fist sweeping towards his right jaw, which he ducked by a whisker. The momentum of Charlie's haymaker knocked him off balance, easing the clamp on Ruby's foot, giving him the chance to counter with a blow to the side of large-belly's head. Ruby's fist bounced off the neanderthal skull, and did more harm to his arm than Charlie's head. Another man would have reeled under the blow, but Charlie took it in his stride and waded back in. He grabbed Ruby by the throat. Breath was squeezed from his lungs. Luckily, Charlie's massive weight when added to Ruby's proved too much for the hitch rail and it snapped. They crashed on to the saloon porch. The unexpected freefall loosened Charlie's stranglehold on Ruby's throat. He gained precious seconds of air into his lungs. Ruby wriggled free and sprang upright, determined not to squander his chance to lay into Charlie. He threw back his arm as far as he could and launched a sweeping pile-driver. This time, avoiding large-belly's rockhard head, he connected with his flabby face in the soft part under his left eye. Frank Ruby felt the soft flesh split and spurting blood greased his fist. His fist slid across Charlie's cheek to make shattering contact with his nose, snapping the bone. Dazed, Charlie swept away the red cloud of blood blinding his eyes as Ruby's next iron-hard blow rained in, punishing further the exact same spot, scoring a raw and ragged wound on Charlie's face. He was cross-eyed. Ruby shelved any trace of mercy, and followed through with a flashing series of punishing blows to the gut. The only interruption to the silence which had taken hold was the fleshy sound of tissue and skin being pulped. Winded, Ruby stepped back.

'Had enough?' he snarled.

His concentration on Charlie, Ruby did not see the flash of a blade in the hand of one of his cohorts to the side of him. The knife was ready to be launched when a bullet whipped the blade from the sneak-knifeman's grasp. The spinning knife almost completed the man's intention anyway, corkscrewing past Ruby inches from his face to embed itself in a support beam of the saloon porch.

Incensed, Ruby spun around.

'Forget it, mister!'

Frank Ruby's angry grey eyes locked with the man wearing the marshal's star. 'I've got right on my side, Marshal,' he growled.

'Won't say that you haven't,' the lawman conceded. 'But you've also got fault on your side.'

'Fault?' Ruby challenged, hotly.

'Sure. Coming into town dressed in that tunic.'

'It's all I've got to wear,' Ruby flung back. 'You Yankees destroyed or pillaged everything else.'

'Better if you rode in buck naked,' was the marshal's opinion, 'than reminding folk of what they've suffered at the hands of Reb raiders.'

'Maybe he was even one of them Reb scum,' said a bitter-faced man loading a buckboard outside the general store, reaching for a rifle under the buckboard's seat.

'Settle down, Hanson,' the marshal warned. 'Wearing grey is obnoxious to us, but a lot of men thought that it was the right thing to do.'

'You taking this bastard's side, Ned?' the man he had addressed as Hanson asked, his face crimped with anger.

'Sounds like it to me,' the knife-thrower snarled.

The marshal's fist shot out to stagger the knife-thrower.

'Now you all listen, and listen good,' the lawman growled. 'I wear a badge that says I've got to protect all men, even those wearing grey,' he emphasized. 'Because all men are free and equal citizens. And whether I like or dislike a man for any reason, he'll still get my protection when the odds are stacked against him.'

'If you'll do that fair and square, Marshal, then you're a better man than most,' Frank Ruby opined.

'I won't always get it right,' the marshal said, 'but I'll damn well try.' He addressed the man called Charlie, Ruby's protagonist. 'Koontz, this is over and done with. Is that understood?'

Charlie Koontz glowered sullenly, hate dancing in his black marble eyes. 'You should know better than to back a Reb agin your own kind, Marshal.'

'It ain't a matter of kind or kin, Charlie,' Ryan stated bluntly. He turned to Koontz's coterie. 'You fellas go on home, if you've got anyone to take you in.' Then it was Frank Ruby's turn. 'And you, follow me.'

The marshal turned towards the jail.

'Am I under arrest?' Frank Ruby questioned.

'You will be if you keep mouthing-off,' the lawman growled. 'Just follow me.'

On reaching the law office, the marshal went straight to a press in the corner from which he took a black suit. He threw it for Ruby to grab.

'Should about fit, I reckon,' he commented.

Ruby examined the cut of the suit. 'Expensive,' was his verdict.

'Belonged to a gambler who thought that he was smarter than everyone else round the poker table. Hope you won't mind too much the bullet hole in the jacket that told him he was not.'

'I don't like wearing a dead man's clothes, Marshal.' Ruby placed the gambler's outfit on the desk. 'I'll be just fine as I am.'

'No, you won't. Did you take a slug in the head? Riding through this territory sporting Confederate grey is going to bring more lead your way than came your way in the war. Put the gambler's duds on, or stay in jail until you change your mind, mister,' was Ryan's ultimatum. 'I don't want a man going to the gallows for you. And neither do I want your neck stretched for someone else's death.'

Frank Ruby grinned. 'You're determined to take good care of me, aren't you, Marshal?'

'Good care of you fiddly!' the lawman grunted. 'Flying lead kills men. That means trouble. And I'm the kind of man who likes to tend my roses, instead of riding the skin off my ass trying to stop another shooting war, when one's just finished.'

'Jail, huh?' Ruby murmured.

'Until that tunic falls off your back from old age,' the marshal promised.

'In that case . . . ' Ruby picked up the gambler's suit. 'Got somewhere I can change?'

Marshal Ned Ryan laughed. 'Why, Reb? You got something different to what I've got?'

'Nothing different, Marshal,' Ruby chirped, 'but maybe bigger. And I wouldn't want to make you jealous.'

'You've got sass, Reb, that's for sure,' Ryan chuckled. 'Through that door behind you, you'll find a cell.'

'No peeking now,' Ruby jibed.

'If a smart mouth could have won the war for the South,' the lawman called after Ruby, 'grey would be the colour right throughout this country.' Ned Ryan went and sat behind his desk. A slow smile spread across his weather-lined face. 'Reb smartass,' he muttered.

A couple of minutes later, Frank Ruby presented himself for inspection.

Ryan opined, 'Somehow those duds don't look the same on you as they did on that gambler. Makes you look like an undertaker.'

Ruby sniffed at the cloth. 'An undertaker with a dove's scent.'

Ned Ryan grinned wryly. 'A man can't play cards all the time. What's your handle, fella?'

'Ruby. Frank Ruby.'

'And what's your business in these parts?'

'Come to visit a lady called Sarah Crockett,' Ruby informed the lawman.

Astonished, the marshal asked, 'In grey?'

'Sarah is a Virginian like me, Marshal. She'd — '

'Blast you out of the saddle,' Ryan interjected. 'It's been less than a year since she buried her husband Walter. A former Yankee officer who got a bullet in the spine in the first months of the war. Sat out the rest of it, a cripple. Days before the end of the war, Reb raiders led by a devil's disciple called Yancey Clark, came by to commandeer fresh horses. Crockett objected. Clark shot him down like a mangy dog.'

The news pained Ruby. And it was pain added to pain as the bitterness of the past flooded back. 'I didn't know that Walter was dead. Nor crippled either.'

Ryan studied Ruby with new interest. Ruby satisfied the marshal's curiosity.

'Sarah's my baby sister.'

'A Dixie Belle hitched to a Yankee!'

'When Sarah married Walter Crockett war clouds had been gathering and tempers were frayed. A Southern gal marrying an avowed Yankee did not go down well with kith or kin.

'Now if I'm not under arrest, I'd like to have that drink I'm thirsting for and hit the trail, Marshal.'

'Not in the saloon you won't,' Ryan stated brusquely. 'This town suffered a lot in the war at the hands of Reb raiders. And a lot of families hereabouts are still mourning the loss of loved ones. Emotions in this town are raw, Ruby; too raw for a Reb to swagger about.'

The marshal opened a desk drawer and extracted a bottle of whiskey, uncorked it and poured it into two tin cups. He handed one of the cups to Frank Ruby.

'That'll slake your thirst as good as any snake's piss that you'll get served up in the saloon.'

Ruby accepted the tin cup and swished its contents about. 'What if I still say that it's a man's right to sup where he wants to sup, Marshal?'

Ned Ryan considered Frank Ruby for a long spell before answering.

'Rights, huh. That's a real rib-tickler coming from a Southerner.'

Frank Ruby reacted angrily. 'The Ruby plantation had no slaves, Marshal. And if you Yankees gave good men in the South the chance the slaves would have been freed and the carnage of the Civil War would never have happened.

'And keep your damn whiskey!'

Ruby slammed the tin cup of whiskey back on Ryan's desk. The Watts Ridge marshal calmly considered Ruby for a long spell until his temper eased. Then he picked up the tin cup and offered it back to Ruby.

'You can drink it or spill it, Reb, but if you spill it, you're leaving this town thirstier than when you arrived.'

The last of Frank Ruby's temper evaporated. He accepted the whiskey and drank.

'What Union outfit did you serve with, Marshal?' he asked.

'None,' came the laconic answer.

'You sat it out?' Ruby asked, disparagingly.

'My roots are Irish, Ruby,' the lawman explained calmly. 'We've fought too many wars for too many stupid reasons, and nothing ever got solved. I learned a spell ago that a day of war takes a lifetime of talking to set wrongs to right. So I figure that talking first is more sensible.

'Talk is always better than shot and shell, I reckon. And you know what, Ruby? The gents who give the orders to start shooting, never get closer to harm than I am right now to the darn moon!'

'Sometimes a man has to fight for what he thinks is right,' Ruby countered. 'I reckon that there's a mighty fine line between cowardice and pacifism. No offence intended, Marshal.'

'You're surely a lippy sort of fella, Ruby,' Ryan opined. 'I guess we'll have to agree that our differences is what makes us different. Now, where're you planning on bunking down?'

'I was counting on a friendly reception at the livery.'

'Hah! I think you can safely count that out. In fact, I figure that you can safely rule out being under any roof in this town tonight. And you can't sleep rough either. That would be inviting trouble.' He eyed Ruby sombrely. 'So I guess that you'll have to remain here.'

'In jail?' Frank Ruby was shaking his head. 'No thanks, Marshal.'

'Did I say you have a choice?' the lawman growled. He grabbed a ring of keys from a hook behind his desk, overruling Ruby's protestations. 'If you spend the night in jail, you won't get yourself killed. And I won't have to hang a citizen for murder.'

When Ruby's protestation continued, Ryan's six-gun flashed from its holster.

'Move,' he ordered. 'In the morning, well rested, with a good breakfast in your belly, you'll thank me.'

'You reckon?' Ruby said, testily.

'Sure you will. Spending a night in the pokey is better than ending up dead.'

'I can take care of myself,' Ruby assured the marshal.

'I don't doubt that,' Ryan agreed. 'But the thing is, then I'd probably have to hang you for murder.' He snorted. 'That's if you didn't get quick justice at the end of a lynch rope.'

Resigned, Frank Ruby said, 'I guess jail it is.'

'Jail it is,' Ned Ryan confirmed.

2

'The middle cell of the three is the most comfortable,' the marshal told Ruby. He handed him the key. 'Open it yourself.'

Ryan stepped back a couple of paces. Frank Ruby seemed a nice enough fella, for a Reb. But hard learned experience had taught the marshal that wolves in sheep's clothing were pretty common in the West.

'You know, Marshal,' Ryan's guest observed, 'never did much take to being threatened by a six-gun.'

Ryan did not remove his threat.

'Sleep well, Ruby. And be out of town ten minutes after you eat breakfast.'

Ruby grinned. 'Friendly cuss, aren't you.'

'It ain't Southern hospitality, just Yankee practicality.'

21

Ryan made to depart.

'What about some light in here?' Ruby asked. 'An hour or less and it'll be as dark as a mineshaft.'

'Lamp oil costs money,' was Ryan's reply. 'Something Watts Ridge ain't rolling in.'

Ruby heard the click of the lock on the door leading from the cells to the law office. 'A careful man,' he murmured.

Frank Ruby was a man used to open spaces, and soon the claustrophobic confines of the small cell had him regretting that he had not ridden on when he had had the chance. Deep into darkness, Ruby reckoned it to be about midnight when he was woken from a troubled sleep by a shuffling of feet and whispering outside the cell window which had only bars and no glass. The moon, which had earlier given some relieving light, had slipped behind storm clouds and had plunged the cell into total darkness. There was something at the window. It looked like a cloth sack, and it looked like it was wriggling.

Ruby froze as he saw a snake slither from the open neck of the sack. The hissing snake dropped on to the cell floor and quickly slid away.

But where to?

'Marshal,' he called out, 'there's a snake in my cell!'

There was no response. Ryan was probably sound asleep. Ruby stood on the bunk, his eyes frantically searching the darkness. He could hear the snake's slither. But one second it was at the far side of the cell, and the next it was up close. Guessing how close up or how far away the reptile really was, was a deadly game of chance.

Suddenly, Ruby's foot went through the base of the bunk, trapping his leg, leaving it exposed and inviting. He felt searing pain as the jagged edge of the ruptured plank tore his leg.

Blood!

From the darkness he heard the snake's excited slide. The door from the law office was yanked open. Ryan appeared, a lamp held aloft. The snake, head flung back was only inches from Ruby. The marshal's pistol blasted. In the yellow lamp light, Ruby saw the headless rattler bounce off the wall of the cell under the window.

From the alley outside, there was a rush of running feet.

'Thanks,' Ruby said.

'That was a close call,' Ned Ryan said. 'You look pretty tuckered out.'

'That about sums it up,' Ruby said.

Ryan opened the cell door. 'I'll brew some beans. You can spend the rest of the night in the office.' Supping strong black coffee five minutes later, recovering from his close call, Frank Ruby said, 'I reckon you know who was behind that stunt, Marshal.'

'I do, I reckon.'

'Aren't you going to do anything about it?'

'No.'

'Why not?'

'Because to do so would create more

problems than it would solve. No harm's been done. A couple of hours from now you'll be gone.'

'And if harm had been done?' Ruby questioned.

'You'd be just another dead Reb, Ruby.' Reacting to Frank Ruby's critical glare, the lawman went on, 'Look, throwing men in jail because they tried to kill a Reb would mean all sorts of trouble that this town doesn't need. A lawman has to take everything into account. And sometimes, it's a choice between evils.'

Wearily, he finished, 'I'm not proud of having to make choices like this, Ruby, but that's the way it is. Wounds are still too raw for folk to understand about fairness and justice. All they want right now is revenge of one kind or another. And it ain't no different in Virginia or Tennessee or Louisiana.'

Though as angry as a wounded polecat, Frank Ruby could understand Ned Ryan's predicament. If what had happened in Watts Ridge had happened in a town across the Mason — Dixon line, and he were a Yankee, the law there would have taken the same route Ryan had. The problem was, Ruby reckoned, that by the time lawmen could act independently of local sensibilities, the country as a whole would have become lawless. An opinion he expressed to the marshal.

Ned Ryan exchanged whiskey for coffee.

'You know, Reb,' he said, taking a long slug, 'I reckon you've struck the nail on the head at that.'

3

Morning brought no friendlier an attitude to Frank Ruby from the citizens of Watts Ridge. At first light, a baying crowd gathered outside the marshal's office, demanding that he run the Reb out of town without further ado.

'Guess I'll skip breakfast,' Ruby told Ryan. 'Don't reckon that I could eat it with a rope round my neck.'

Ryan said, grittily, 'I'm the damn law in this town, not that mob out there.'

But behind his bluster, Ruby observed a keen sense of relief in the marshal at seeing the back of him. And the sooner the better. He could understand Ned Ryan's anxiety. He was a lone man against a mob with its blood up. If it came down to it, there wasn't much he could do to stop the mob breaking into the jail and hauling his prisoner to the nearest tree — probably the fine oak at the south end of Main which he had passed when he had arrived in town the previous day.

'Thanks for your hospitality, Marshal,' Ruby said. 'Maybe we'll cross paths again some time.'

'Not in this town, I reckon,' the lawman opined.

'Who knows? Life has a fickle way about it, Marshal. Darn stubborn too. Never does what you want it to do.'

'Ain't that a fact,' Ryan sighed.

Frank Ruby stepped out of the marshal's office. The howling mob pressed in on him. Spittle lathered his face as he forced a narrow path through the crowd. A rock struck him on the shoulder, and was no doubt intended for his skull. The last straw. Polecat angry, Ruby swung around in the direction from which the rock had been thrown, his grey eyes blazing.

'Would the coward who threw that rock like to step out?' he challenged. His venom-laced reaction stilled the crowd, and they moved back from him. 'Well?' he growled, his furious gaze scanning the mob for the merest hint of the culprit.

Ned Ryan intervened. 'Best if you let it be,' he told Ruby.

'And if I don't want to?' Ruby flung back.

Ryan leaned into the law office to the gun rack near the door, and came back toting a shotgun. 'Is this answer enough?' he asked Ruby.

'Chances are, Marshal,' Ruby said, 'that I'd clear leather before you could pull those triggers.'

'Maybe you could at that,' Ryan conceded. 'But if you didn't, it would be raining parts of you in Mexico.'

Ruby looked round at the fast retreating crowd. He scowled. 'At least you did something useful, Marshal,' he commented angrily, and walked on to the livery.

Mounted up, Frank Ruby rode out of town past sullen faces, bitter with hatred. The day promised to be the kind of day that Satan would feel hot in. It was only a half-hour after sun-up, but already wave after wave of heat was wilting everything and everyone in its path. It was the kind of day in which a man, if he had sense and if he could, would seek out some shade, a cool beer, and do nothing much but breathe. And that would be the way that the three men, who had decided to follow Frank Ruby with no good intentions, would have spent it, were it not for the hatred that any man who had fought for the Confederacy instilled in them.

They had drifted out of Watts Ridge one by one to meet up outside of town, not wanting anyone to notice their departure as a group. Their mission, being one of murder, they did not want anyone recalling their leaving.

No one had, except one man: Ned Ryan.

The trail out of town was a straight, narrow road with rolling range on either side; country that was pretty much devoid of bushwhacker's cover, and therefore Frank Ruby rode easy in his saddle. He had anticipated that the degree of bitterness in town at his presence would not end on his departure, and that trouble would follow. His disadvantage was his lack of knowledge of the terrain ahead. Often a danger-free trail suddenly merged into less open country. And if trouble was to come, it would come in terrain that offered the kind of cover that bush-whackers needed to do their dirty deeds.

Although the main trail out of town was as yet posing no problems, there would, Ruby knew, be many lesser trails that local men would know about; trails that could put them ahead of him to a place where they could vent their spleen on him.

The men following Frank Ruby had picked their ambushers' lair well — a narrow gorge through a creek about a mile outside of town through which, due to his lack of local knowledge, he would have to pass.

Drawing close to the creek, Ruby slowed his pace. The shady oasis, he reckoned, might be deceptively benign. However, he figured that it would be in the narrow gorge through which the creek flowed beyond its wider basin, where any threat would most likely lurk.

He let his horse pick its own way down the shale track to the creek, making a pose of sitting easy in the saddle while all the time as tense as a clock spring, ready to leap from leather at the slightest hint of trouble.

On reaching the creek, Ruby was careful to go through all of the motions that an unsuspecting traveller would go through: he doused his face and hair with the creek's cool water; watered his horse, but sparingly. A horse with a bellyful of water would not be wise if trouble reared its head and he had to make fast tracks. He filled his canteen, brewed coffee, chewed jerky, sweated a lot, listened a lot, too. He tensed every muscle and hoped that he would get a hint of trouble a split-second before it erupted.

Waited.

Nothing.

Regaining his saddle, Frank Ruby hoped that he had played the role of an unsuspecting traveller with enough perfection to fool any watchers. Often, a man could act all he liked, but there would be some hint or other, maybe in the set of his shoulders or the style of his gait that would warn his enemies.

Ruby rode along the creek into the gorge.

The willowy slopes of the creek gave way to bare rock. Ruby began to whistle tunelessly, the way a man with an idle mind might.

'He's coming,' the leader of the bushwhackers alerted his partners.

'Straight into our guns, too,' a second man said.

The third man growled, 'We'll show that bastard Reb, Jed.'

Jed Hanson turned his hatred-poisoned face to his comrades. 'No mistakes. Wait until he's close enough to kiss before you open up,' he said.

4

Frank Ruby's breath became shorter as he rode deeper into the gorge. It took all his resolve to keep going. Turning back was a mighty attactive option. There were other trails. He'd find them. At another time, with his pride not so dented, he might have sought another way. But since the end of the war, almost every man he came across had wanted him to eat humble pie, and he had had more than enough of backing off. The more a man back-tracked, the easier it became to do so. And every time a little bit of his pride was chipped away, until one day, he wasn't a man any more. From then on he would live his life snivelling and grovelling. The kind of man on whom men cleaned their boots, instead of paying for a doormat. If he came out the other side of the gorge standing, he'd be the stronger man for it. And if he did not, then it would not matter either way.

Ruby tensed. Was that a reflection of sunlight on a gun barrel in the lofty promontory just ahead? Or was it a trick of light? Maybe his nerves, too, were acting up.

The first hint of trouble came when his horse snorted and began to hold back. It was just before heading into the narrowest part of the gorge. Full of nooks and crannies, it was a natural bushwhackers' lair.

'Easy, girl,' Ruby coaxed the mare.

The horse settled some, but remained a reluctant visitor to the narrow track directly ahead. Frank Ruby wondered why, if men were lurking, they had not picked him off? And he thought he knew why. His would-be waylayers were not proficient shooters. That meant that they were likely riled up hotheads who resented their prize being taken from them, or were driven by pure hatred. And their reticence to shoot came from the fact that the closer he got to them, the greater would their chance be of downing him first time. A rash and wild volley would be counter productive and probably fatal, because he would be off his horse and into the rocks in a flash. Then the skirmish would develop into a straight battle of wits with the outcome uncertain.

A vulture circled in the copper sky. Birds were naturally curious creatures. Was the vulture sensing a meal? Or just lazing about in hope?

Ruby had done many difficult things in recent times, but heading into the narrowest section of the gorge was one of the most daunting, because his life could be mere seconds long now.

★   ★   ★

In the rocks, Jed Hanson wiped a lather of sweat from his face. The men with him, too, were on edge. Though they had the advantage, they also knew that the Reb was one tough *hombre* who, if they made a mistake, would show them no mercy. One of the men, the shakiest of the three, even tentatively suggested to Hanson that they might rethink their mission.

'You're not going to go yellow on me, are you, Spike?' Hanson snarled.

'No, I ain't,' the man called Spike, having seen Hanson's rages, hurriedly reassured the trio's leader and motivator. 'It's just that . . . well, I've got Mary and the girls to think about, Jed.'

Hanson's attitude was uncompromising.

'We've all got responsibilities, Spike. But does that mean that we have to let this Reb rub our noses in it?'

'Well, I'm not sure he did that, Jed,' Spike said, shakily, his boldness stemming from a greater fear of catching lead in any confrontation with the Reb than tangling with Hanson. A trashing, though sore, was preferable to a bullet hole.

Hanson was incensed.

'I knew you'd turn yellow! Should

have left you back in town with your knitting.' Jed Hanson turned to the third man of the trio. 'Jack, what've you got to say?'

Jack shrugged and swallowed hard.

'You ain't gone yellow too, have you?' Hanson ranted.

The man called Jack shifted his position uneasily, thought briefly about backing Spike, but cowardice won out.

'No, Jed. O' course not.'

'Then I guess you and me will have to do the man's work 'round here,' Hanson growled. His stare when he looked at Spike was dark and dangerous, and glowering with contempt.

Backing off to his horse, Spike pleaded, 'You've got to understand — '

'Get outa here!' Hanson raged. 'If I ever see your snivelling face again, it'll be too soon for my liking.'

'Hey, Jed,' Jack said urgently. 'Here he comes.'

Hanson looked down from the vulture's perch on which they were bellied down, to watch Frank Ruby riding easy and unconcerned in the saddle. Gleefully he pronounced, 'Doesn't suspect a thing.'

'I'll see you fellas back in town,' Spike said.

'I've changed my mind. You're staying put, Spike,' Hanson commanded. 'Any movement now could alert the Reb.'

Spike's budding protest was cut short by the trio's leader.

'You heard what I said.'

'Sure, Jed,' Spike said, bereft of the courage to stand up to Hanson's bullying.

'Now, we ain't the best shots in the territory,' Hanson said, 'so we don't shoot 'til he's close enough to look him in the eye. Understand?'

Jack and Spike nodded, exchanging fear-filled glances when Hanson resumed his perusal of Frank Ruby's steady progress towards them.

'I'm going to enjoy seeing lead in that Reb bastard's gut,' Jed Hanson said.

5

Ruby's ears pricked up at the sound of a pebble skittering between the rocks. Man or beast? he wondered. Or maybe it was just the natural settling of the rocks? He was well into the gorge by now and had seen no sign of trouble. He was beginning to think that the trouble in town had made him more edgy than he'd care to admit. He had had trouble in towns like Watts Ridge before. But then it had been men letting off steam, and mostly drunken steam at that. However, the trouble in Watts Ridge had a nasty edge to it that was a long way from any he had experienced before.

The kind of trouble that flared to a killing lust.

★   ★   ★

41

Jed Hanson rebuked the man called Spike.

'Can't you sit still!'

'Sorry, Jed,' Spike apologized. 'My boot slipped.'

Hanson turned to check Ruby's route. He was still on target. It looked like the sliding pebble had not alerted him to danger. But Hanson was not counting on that. The Reb had been through a war in which a man had needed sharp instincts to survive.

'Keep right on coming, Reb,' Hanson murmured.

★ ★ ★

Frank Ruby drew rein, took off his hat and wiped the sweat from his brow. The innocent-looking action was one he had used many times to scan his surroundings. In the last couple of seconds, the hair on the back of his neck had begun to tingle. It was a warning which he had heeded in the past, and he had survived an onslaught of one kind or another by trusting his instincts. He would heed it again now.

He wondered if he should risk a full gallop through the remainder of the narrow gorge?

★　★　★

'He's stopped,' Hanson fretted.

'Only to wipe the sweat from his brow, Jed,' the man called Jack said.

Spike, whose courage was completely gone now, began edging towards his horse while his partners concentrated on the Reb.

'Maybe we should try and down him right now?' was Jack's suggestion.

Hanson had been thinking along the same lines, but was fearful that if he missed his target, Ruby would run for cover and present them with a problem which just might be beyond their capability to deal with.

'Well, Jed?' Jack urged, his finger itchy on his rifle trigger. 'I figure I could get him from here.' After some more

consideration, Jed Hanson decided.
'We wait.'

★ ★ ★

Ruby tried to chart a reasonably safe track for a galloping horse to follow, but saw how useless an exercise it was. There was hardly a foot of rock-free terrain. Most of the rocks were spiked or jagged, and would rip a horse's leg open. There was also a liberal helping of loose stones and shale on which a galloping horse could slip. The sensible thing would be to turn back. He had already decided against that option. But had he made the right decision? If he changed his mind would he make it, exposed as he was to a bushwhacker's bullet? Would it not though be sensible to live to fight another day?

Frank Ruby silently rebuked himself, and chased away the creeping temptation that would have him believe that turning his back one more time would be the last time he would do so. He had already walked away from trouble too many times, in the hope that trouble would sooner or later walk away from him. Trouble never had. Trouble never would. Trouble, like fear, had to be mastered before it became a monster that stalked your every waking moment.

'No more backing-off!' he grated.

But he could turn and hope to draw hasty fire which would pinpoint their location.

* * *

'Shit!' Jed Hanson swore. 'He's turning back.'

On hearing this news, Spike, who was about to swing into the saddle and hightail it, decided that he could save face and not risk Hanson's wrath by staying where he was, pretending that he'd have been whole-heartedly with his partners had the Reb kept coming. In his rush, his six-gun got tangled on his lariat and tumbled out of its holster. He grabbed for the gun; fouled up.

Hamfisted, his thumb cocked the hammer. The six-gun bounced off a boulder. Primed, the gun exploded. The blast echoed through the gorge. The wild bullet buzzed off another boulder. Chips from the boulder sprayed out. Unlucky, Jack caught one on the back of the leg. More unlucky, Spike caught one in the right eye: a thin, pointed missile that pierced his brain. Jack howled. Spike sighed. Jack, wounded, was pretty much useless to Hanson. There was no question but that Spike was beyond help and beyond usefulness.

'Stay down!' Hanson hollered desperately, when Jack leapt up in a crazy dance.

A rifle cracked.

Jack grabbed his chest and pitched forward into the lower reaches of the gorge.

The odds were evened.

Hanson against the Reb.

And the Reb was nowhere to be seen!

6

Frank Ruby had taken advantage of the confusion in the bushwhackers' camp to dive into the rocks immediately below their perch. But his action was not of much help. The assassins had chosen well. Their lofty lair would be impossible to get near without incurring the serious risk of them completing their murderous task. And now on foot, he'd make by far an easier target than he would have made aboard a galloping horse.

His choices were stark: he could sit out the siege in the hope of getting a lucky break, but the furnace sun, more intense than ever in the tight hollow he was in, would take its toll, or he could flush out the ambushers, or perhaps ambusher? There had been some kind of trouble in the killers' camp, but how serious or how much of an advantage it was to him could not be ascertained. The problem was that his choices would be known to the bushwhackers, because they were more or less shared. However, he had the consolation of knowing that the heat on the high ground would be intense and punishing also. But a breeze, still feather-light, which had begun to blow, would tip the scales in his opponents' favour should it strengthen.

Trapped, and with the noon sun beating down on him, the odds began to mount against Frank Ruby. There were aces in the deck, but it wasn't at all clear yet to whom they would fall.

★   ★   ★

Jed Hanson had jitters. His partners were dead. The Reb had vanished. The only plus was the high ground his hidey-hole occupied. The Reb would not find it easy to reach him, without taking risks. On the other hand, a sitting target often got picked off. Maybe he should try and reach the Reb, instead of letting him dictate the terms of the encounter. How good or bad a tactician might he be? He knew how good with a rifle he was. He had only had a glimpse of Jack Mallard, and Mallard was dead. What would his resistance to the blistering sun be? Better than his? Should he hightail it while he still had a chance?

Hightail it be damned!

Hanson's hatred and bitterness for any man who had fought for the Confederacy would override all else. Reb raiders led by Yancey Clark, Satan's spawn, had raped and murdered his wife only days before the war had ended. And since that evil day he had devoted his time to killing as many Rebs as he could, until the ransom for Martha Hanson's death had been collected — if ever it was.

★   ★   ★

It was a stand-off.

But the problem with a stand-off, Ruby knew, was that sooner or later someone would have to make a move to break it. And that someone would carry the lion's share of the risk. He licked parched lips, and looked longingly at the canteen tied to his horse's saddle horn, and then to the blazing orb of the sun. It also worried him that his horse stood exposed and totally vulnerable. He called to the mare. The horse just stood and looked, dumbly.

'So much for horse sense!' Ruby muttered.

★　★　★

Hanson crept round the pot-bellied boulder he was biding behind. He was risking a degree of exposure, but he had to try and get some idea of where the Reb was. The stand-off would probably be broken long before dark, but if it were not, the advantage would lie with the Reb, an experienced soldier.

50

On seeing Ruby's horse, and the canteen tied to its saddle horn, Hanson's spirits lifted considerably. He drew a bead on the horse.

'Try and make it out of here without a horse and water, Reb,' he growled.

* * *

The instant Frank Ruby heard the crack of Hanson's rifle, he knew that his worst fears had been confirmed. The horse staggered. A second shot and the mare folded. The mare's weight crushed the canteen. Its contents spilled into the sandy soil.

A man without a horse and water was a dead man walking.

7

An hour had gone by. A blistering hour in which Frank Ruby, exposed as he was to the sun's full intensity, had felt the energy being sucked out of him. He would enjoy no reprieve from the sun's debilitating effects for a long time yet. Meanwhile, a high rockface towering over the ambushers' perch, would give it shade probably an hour before it brought any relief to him.

No water. No horse. Deadly sun.

Undertaker's bait.

★　★　★

Jed Hanson strained to get a glimpse of the Reb, but he had to be careful not to overreach. He had witnessed in Jack Mallard's demise how handy with a rifle the Reb was. He didn't need much of a sighting to make a telling shot.

Poke his head out an inch, and it might be an inch too far.

*   *   *

Ruby was quick to spot a puff of dust drift off the high ground where his would-be killer was lurking; dust that maybe a crawling man would unsettle. He edged sideways, rifle at the ready should a target present itself. The problem was that in trying for a shooting angle to nail his assassin, he would also make himself more visible.

*   *   *

Hanson caught a glimpse of a boot heel in a hollow almost directly below him. At the same time Ruby spotted the brim of a Stetson above him. Hanson wondered if he might risk exposure to try for a disabling shot to maim the Reb's leg, while Ruby pondered on the risk of showing himself to try and deliver a bullet to the head inside the Stetson.

Seconds ticked.

Frank Ruby made up his mind. He would act now. There was no way, tiring and parched as he was, that he could hold out indefinitely. He would take the initiative and the risks that went with it. But he was not a gambler. He was a planner by nature and by training. Therefore, though the temptation to try for a lucky shot that might end the stand-off in his favour was overwhelming, he chose the less spectacular option of flushing out the bushwhacker.

It would be slow, tedious work — one boulder, one rock at a time. Every second laden with the risk of sudden and bloody death.

As he began his slow crawl upwards to the bushwhackers' lair, Frank Ruby wondered, if for once, he should have pitched caution to the wind and gone for a bold gesture.

His mind drifted back to the war . . .

8

Though having saved many lives in the war, Frank Ruby's caution had worked against him when compared to more flamboyant but less able colleagues who had outstripped him in rank, many of whom had not cared how they had achieved their successes, or how many men had died to bring them glory. The fact was, that in military circles, the outlandish successes which could have been disastrous failures had good fortune not played its part in their outcome, were remembered when promotions were being handed out. Politicians liked to bask in the sunshine of victory, and senior officers liked to please their political masters. That was their road to the upper echelons of both civil and military society.

The fighting men liked officers of Captain Frank Ruby's calibre, who put

55

their welfare into the equation when decisions were being made. But they would prefer, if they survived, to be among the ranks of men commanded by officers who were hailed as military geniuses, even though their status had been achieved on a fortunate twist of fate rather than sound military strategy. In essence, all wars were won by the officers and men who planned every day, rather than by the flash-in-the-pan officers who sought personal and individual glory, often at the expense of overall victory.

One such man had been Yancey Clark, who, if he had not taken that final risk against the odds, might have ended the war as a hero. Instead he had taken one risk too many which had backfired, resulting in heavy losses and a Union breakthrough, and he had been drummed out in disgrace. The pity was that had he chosen to reach the senior rank he craved by fair means, there was no doubt but that he would have got it. He just did not have the patience to earn glory, preferring to steal it instead.

Frank Ruby and Yancey Clark had been boys together and firm friends going into the war. But as Clark had taken outrageous risk after risk their paths had divided, and they had become implacable enemies. Clark's quest for glory at a sometimes terrible cost, had appalled Frank Ruby.

★　★　★

Ruby, on his belly, was crawling up through the rocks inch by inch. Flat on the ground, he reduced greatly the risk of being picked off. However, the punishing slow crawl, as opposed to a quick sprint, quickly burned up his reserves of energy. But the whole purpose of the exercise was to gain higher ground undetected. Therefore stealth and patience were the best tools.

He had thought about risking a run to a ridge in an off-shoot of the gorge the prominence of which would about match that of the ambushers' lair, but there was a long track of rocky ground which offered little cover and lots of problems in its precarious conditions underfoot. A fall could break bones and leave him helpless. And, running, his shooting would be purely unaimed cover fire. Ruby figured that if he got a clear shooting opportunity, he would have to be close enough to make it count. He had already felled one of the bush-whackers. But he could not again count on a lucky shot, because that was surely what it had been.

Steadily, nursing every pebble on the steeply rising track, Frank Ruby clawed his way upwards. He paused to draw breath and wipe the sweat from his eyes. He was half way up the track and, to his amazement, had gone undetected.

Or had he?

His gaze went to the blind curve in the trail ahead. What was beyond? Would the ambushers have a clear sight of him? Might they be waiting for him to show? Enjoying every second of his torturous crawl up the track?

Suddenly, Frank Ruby had a sense of eyes watching him. Overwrought imagination, perhaps? He scanned the way ahead and also the terrain around and behind him. Nothing. Should he lie perfectly still? Or should he dive for the deeper cover at the side of the track? Either option had its risks. Lying still would make him a sitting target. And sliding off the track could not be achieved without unsettling shale. However, there was a third option and that was to continue on his slow crawl, and hope that if someone was watching him he would present a reasonably difficult target to hit.

It was a devil's choice, he faced.

9

Deciding on continuing with his slow crawl, Ruby strained to pick up the slightest sound or the merest hint of movement, hoping that he would get a half-chance to defend himself. Every muscle in his body was taut with tension — too taut. Tension was good, but too much tension would be counter-productive, and would sap his muscles of the flexibility he would need to react if a surprise lay in waiting.

Ruby's luck deserted him. Just as he rounded the curve in the track, its fragile edge crumbled. He clawed at the loose stones spilling off the track, but felt them run through his fingers. They clattered off the rocks and boulders below the track, sounding to Ruby's ears like stones rattling in an empty bucket.

Alerted, Jed Hanson sprang on top of

a boulder. He had the Reb in his gunsights. It was an easy shot. But fortunately for Frank Ruby, in his anxiety to make the kill, Hanson hurried his shot. Though the bullet was uncomfortably close, it buzzed harmlessly past. Ruby returned fire. The bushwhacker clutched at his left shoulder and spun off the boulder. Ruby, knowing that he had only seconds, raced up the track. Hanson, who had fallen heavily and awkwardly was just about regaining his wind when he glanced up into the barrel of Ruby's rifle.

'Twitch and you're dead!' Ruby snarled.

Seething but helpless, Jed Hanson let his rifle clatter to the stony ground. 'Go on!' he yelled. 'Kill me! Don't matter none to me now. Ain't been nothing worth living for since you bastards raped and murdered my Martha.'

'Martha?'

'My wife.' He heaped scorn and hatred on Ruby. 'Mebbe you were one of them devils yourself?'

Ruby, though ready to kill Hanson seconds before, was now moved to pity by the man's anguish. 'I've never been in these parts before yesterday, mister. And,' he said sombrely, 'I'd remind you that the Yankees did as much raping and murdering as the Confederates.'

'You expect me to believe that?' Hanson raged.

'Guess not,' Ruby said. 'At least not while you're hurting the way you are. But later, when your pain and hurt eases — '

'It never will!'

'You might see the logic and sense of what I've said,' Ruby finished.

'Kill me!' Hanson screamed. 'You'll be doing me a favour, Reb.'

'And give you the chance to spend eternity thinking that you were right, and that all Dixie boys are rapists and killers? No way am I going to do that.'

Frank Ruby knew that he was taking one hell of a chance. He placed his rifle on the ground. The bushwhacker was a big, raw-boned man whose body would pack a tornado of power should he choose to tackle him. Hanson's eyes were puzzled by Ruby's action, his hate-filled perception of all Rebs scattered like straw in a gale.

'I'd be obliged if I could have your horse though, given freely,' Ruby said. 'You see, if I take one of your partners' nags, they not being able to give their permission, someone might figure that I was a horse-thief. And I sure as hell have enough problems right now without that added to my woes.'

'You're not going to shoot me down like a dog?' Hanson checked, baffled.

'No.'

'But I'd have killed you,' Hanson said, his puzzlement deepening.

Frank Ruby sighed. 'Isn't it about time that the killing stopped? And someone's got to stop first. Now about that horse?'

Hanson nodded, and pointed.

'Thanks.'

Ruby was vaulting into the saddle

when he heard a rifle being primed behind him. He turned slowly. Hanson, rifle on him, laughed bitterly.

'Knew Rebs were cowardly rapists and killers, but I never figured they were dumb as well.'

Frank Ruby stood stock still and held Hanson's gaze.

'Are you planning on killing me in cold blood?' he enquired of the bushwhacker.

'Well, now that I've got you cold, I'm sure not going to give you the chance to kill me, Reb!'

'Kind of proves my point, doesn't it?'

'What point would that be?' Jed Hanson growled.

'That maybe some Yankees are as cold-blooded killers as some Rebs are.'

Shaken, Hanson's anger fizzled out as he accepted Frank Ruby's argument. After a long time he lowered the rifle to his side.

'Thanks for the horse,' Ruby said.

He mounted up and rode away.

★ ★ ★

With evening shadows closing in, Frank Ruby stopped at a shallow creek to prepare a meagre meal. His brush with the bushwhackers had stymied his progress, and he had decided that he would stop overnight and complete the journey to his sister's farm on the morrow. Riding in the dark was a dangerous pastime for man and beast, but arriving unannounced at a homestead in such troubled and perilous times would be foolhardy in the extreme. The likelihood was that his sister, nervous as she must be, would blast him out of the saddle before he got a chance to declare himself. She was a widow, alone, in a land full of men whose natures had been made raw by war and bloodshed, some of whom were no better than wild animals; predators whose only consideration was their own survival or pleasure.

He had not seen Sarah for three years; hard years that would have taken their toll on her as they had on him. But even having suffered life's cruel twists and turns, Sarah had beauty, grace and poise in such an abundance that even now she would still be a desirable woman; the kind of woman who would prove a lure for the kind of men who preyed on women.

Ruby's mind drifted back to happier times and Sarah's laughter filled his head, the strains too of an orchestra. The scene he was recalling was his sister's farewell ball. It had not been a night to remember. The only guests who had attended had been staunch family friends who pitied Charles Ruby for having a daughter who was about to wed a Yankee.

War was not yet certain. Some hoped that the Union could be talked round. Others had accepted the inevitability of war, some were even eager for it, and were already seeing men like Walter Crockett as enemies of the Confederacy. As were any Southerners who chose to seek the company of a Yankee.

Charles Ruby had been uneasy with his daughter's choice of husband, and had hoped right to the end that Sarah would see sense and marry wisely. He had not wanted to break his daughter's heart by banishing Walter Crockett. But that night, in a confidence shared with Frank Ruby, he had bitterly bemoaned his lack of courage and wisdom.

'There'll be two houses within the one, Frank,' he had fretted. 'And Sarah will be living in Yankee territory.'

He had tried as best he could to assuage his father's fears. But, troubled himself, he had proved to be an unconvincing comforter.

The ensuing years saw the demise of the South in the slaughter and ruins of conflict. But Sarah's desertion and betrayal, as Charles Ruby had come to see his beloved daughter's marriage to a Yankee, was for him the most bitter blow of all; a blow that finally laid him low.

The snap of a twig jerked Frank Ruby out of his reverie. Alert, though he did not tense a single telltale muscle, he remained seated at the small fire and reached for the coffee pot as if he did not have a care in the world. A man at ease in himself.

Ruby's ears followed the sound, trying to pin it down. He reckoned that the sound had come from the far bank of the creek. His reasoning was based on the fact that as the sound travelled, there was a sliver of a second's clarity of pitch that suggested that the sound had crossed over the water of the creek, before again taking on the muted tone induced by the creek's luxuriant vegetation.

In the war, his ears had often been as useful as a weapon, giving him the hint of an enemy's presence a second before he became a deadly threat. It was a sense which Frank Ruby had worked hard on tuning and perfecting.

Who might his visitor be? He might be an innocent traveller, or he could be a wily predator. In troubled times a man would be wise to be cautious before walking uninvited into another man's camp. The wise man watched and waited for a spell, before making his move. Of course, the danger was that an evil-doer might behave in exactly the same way as an innocent.

Ruby waited. There wasn't much else he could do. He was counting on the fact that if his visitor meant him harm, he would already have tried to inflict it on him.

When the man walked out of the shadows, near enough to where Ruby reckoned he had been, it gave him a feeling of satisfaction that he had guessed right. However, the shadowy figure also gave him a sense of apprehension; a sense that vanished as soon as the man spoke.

'Ain't made much progress have you, Ruby?' Ned Ryan, the Watts Ridge marshal crossed the creek. 'That coffee hot and strong?' His next question was, 'Are you finished with that tin cup?'

Ruby handed over the cup.

Ryan rinsed it with coffee, filled the cup again and hunkered down at the fire. 'Figured you took a mite too long to deal with those bushwhackers,' the Watts Ridge lawman opined. Ruby recalled the feeling of eyes on him as he made his way up the track to the ambushers' perch. Reading Ruby's thoughts, Ned Ryan said, 'I figured that you had the measure of Hanson and his cronies. But I'd have stepped in if it looked like you hadn't, Reb. Had a clear shot from that ridge you were contemplating on trying for. You'd never have made it across open ground though.'

He continued to answer Frank Ruby's unspoken questions.

'Saw them leave town on your tail. It wasn't hard, even for a clunkhead like me to put two and two together to get four.'

Ruby thought that Ned Ryan was a long way off being a clunkhead.

'Said I'd tag along for a spell, just in case. You being a mighty unpopular fella round these parts, someone else might have had the same thought as Hanson.'

'Obliged, Marshal,' Ruby drawled.

'Was right, too.'

The lawman's remark made Ruby sit up. Ryan walked back across the creek to the slope and hauled an unconscious man out of the bushes.

'Had you in his sights, just as I happened along. Name's Tom Carver. Lost his whole family in a Reb raid. He'll have a sore head for a day or two when he wakes up.' Ryan smiled. 'That twig you heard snap . . . Tom.'

'Thanks for the favour.'

Ryan said, 'No favour, Ruby. Just doing my job.'

'Thanks anyway.'

'Mind if I bed down for the night?' Ryan asked.

'It's free country, Marshal. But I haven't got much grub that I can offer you.'

'What you've got will do just fine.'

'No objection to eating Reb jerky and

Dixie biscuits?' Ruby asked, with a wry smile.

Ryan's smile was equally wry. 'Not if you don't mind Yankee company.'

The man whom Ryan had laid out with a clip of his six-gun butt stirred, woke and squinted at the marshal.

'You near busted my skull,' he accused Ryan.

'A small price to pay for what you had in mind, Carver,' the marshal flung back.

Gathering his wits, Carver growled, 'Never knew you was a Reb lover, Marshal.'

'I'm a lawman,' Ryan said sternly. 'And murder is murder, Carver.'

Carver declared angrily, 'Killin' a Reb ain't no murder!'

Ryan whistled and his horse came across the creek. He took his lariat and cut off a length of the rope. 'On your belly,' he ordered Carver.

Carver's eyes, mean to start with, narrowed further. His resentment was palpable.

'Shacklin' me to save a Reb's hide ain't goin' to go down well back in town,' he snarled. 'In fact, folk might see it as a mighty unfriendly thing to do, Marshal.'

'Maybe they will, maybe they won't,' Ryan said. 'Now, on your belly!'

Left with no choice, Carver grudgingly obeyed. 'This isn't the end of this,' he threatened.

Trussed, Ryan hauled him to a tree and sat him against it. Returning to sit near Ruby, he partook of the sparrow's meal on offer.

'Want some?' Ruby asked Carver.

He spat in the dust. 'Reb grub. I ain't that hungry.'

'It'll be a long and hungry night, Tom,' Ryan said.

'I'll survive,' Carver growled. 'I'll make sure of that. I've got a tale to tell and a job to finish.'

The next couple of hours were spent in pleasant conversation with Ned Ryan, during which time Frank Ruby's opinion of the marshal as a fair-minded and impartial lawman was enhanced. Before turning in, both men had shared a lot of pleasurable moments, watched by an increasingly hostile Tom Carver.

'Time to turn in, I guess,' Ruby finally said.

'Expect me to sleep with my hands tied behind my back, Ryan?' Carver berated the lawman.

Ryan said, unsympathetically, 'Your position is of your own making, Tom.'

The night passed without incident. At first light, Ruby took his leave of the marshal.

'Give my regards to your sister, Ruby,' Ryan said. 'A fine woman, your sister.'

It was probably a trick of light, but Ruby could have sworn that he had seen a warm glow in Ned Ryan's eyes when he spoke of Sarah.

'I sure will, Marshal,' Ruby assured him.

★　★　★

Mid-morning, Frank Ruby crested a hill overlooking his sister's farm. The house looked deserted. He fretted that she might have moved on. But wouldn't Ryan have known if that were so? Maybe not. Although the distance between Watts Ridge and the farm was not that great, in the West it was considerable. Then his worries were put at ease when he saw Sarah struggling with a stubborn plough horse, alternately coaxing and scolding it towards the plough. His smile faded. He was some distance off, but it was obvious that life had not been kind to Sarah. Her movements were not as free and co-ordinated as he remembered. She moved wearily, and her natural grace had given way to a stolidness that he could never have imagined even a short few years ago. She had all the hallmarks of a woman alone and struggling. As he rode up, it saddened him to see her worn appearance. The red flaming hair had lost its lustre and now straggled rather than bounced, and it was liberally streaked with grey. Her soft skin had been hardened by the blistering sun, and her faded blue eyes reflected an ocean of hard times.

She watched Ruby ride towards her, backing off a little as he drew nearer, her glance going nervously to the rifle standing against the cabin wall.

'Sarah,' he called. 'It's me, Frank.'

'Frank?' she questioned doubtfully, shading her eyes.

'I guess I've changed some too, Sis,' he chuckled.

As he dismounted, she ran to meet him, throwing her arms round his neck and holding him as tight as she could. His heart stung at the sound of her woeful sobbing. There was nothing to say. After a while, she took his hand and led him inside the house and set about preparing a meal. No words passed between them until the meal was on the table. Then Frank said, 'You look tuckered out, Sarah.'

She smiled sadly. 'I'm no spring

chicken any more, Brother.' Self-consciously, she tucked in the loose strands of hair that hung down limply on her cheeks. 'Besides, you're looking kind of worn yourself.'

Ruby chuckled. 'I'd preferred to think of myself as being tattered, Sis. But redeemable.'

'Is there a difference between tattered and tuckered?'

'I guess not.'

'That meat pie needs eating pretty fast,' Sarah cautioned. 'It's been reheated twice before.'

'It's fine,' he reassured her.

Another silence settled between them, each one getting longer. Ruby had never imagined that it would be this way. He had thought that on seeing each other the years separating them would have melted away and it would be as if they had never been. The war wouldn't matter. Sarah's marriage to a Yankee wouldn't matter. Their father's premature death wouldn't matter. The fact that a whole way of life had vanished wouldn't matter. But he was learning that the bridges burned would take time to rebuild.

'The farm must be a lot of hard work for a woman alone, Sarah,' Ruby said.

'Farming in dry country is hard for man, woman or beast, Frank. Not at all like the lush pastures and fat stock of a plantation,' she said, wistfully.

She looked at Ruby, sadness stalking her blue eyes.

'Sometimes I dream about it, you know. Home.'

'It's gone, Sarah,' Ruby said bluntly. 'Burned down by the Ya — '

Sarah's gaze went to a framed picture of Walter Crockett on the dresser, wearing the uniform of a Union captain.

'Bad times for everyone, I guess, Frank,' she sighed.

Ruby nodded. 'Over now though.'

'Are they?' she asked, wearily. 'The killing is. But the bitterness will linger well beyond our time, I reckon.'

'And what about between you and

me, Sarah?' he asked, quietly.

Sarah smiled. 'I wish you no ill-will, Frank. But there's no denying the past is there. I chose where I stood, and never regretted my choice. Walter was a fine man. Maybe not as bookish, as learned and as finely mannered as a Southern gent, but he loved me, Frank.' Tears welled up in her eyes. 'And I loved him like I could never love any other man.'

Suddenly angry, Sarah swept away the half-eaten meat pie.

'You can't eat that now.'

He grabbed her hand. 'It's fine, Sarah.' She tried to break free, but he held her steadfast. 'Want me to leave? Maybe it would be best.'

'Maybe,' she said. 'Maybe too much has happened for us to ever be friends again, Frank.'

He stood up from the table. 'If that's what you want, Sarah.'

'You'll need to rest awhile,' Sarah said, when Frank was at the door.

'I'll rest under the clouds or stars,

Sarah. It's what I've been doing since the end of the war.' He continued on out, crossed the yard to his horse, mounted up and rode away. Some way off he glanced back. Sarah was again struggling with the stubborn plough horse. He was tempted to return, but Sarah was right. Too much had happened for them to ever be the kind of friends they had been growing up.

'Damn the war!' he swore, and fixed his eyes unwaveringly on the trail ahead.

A while later, Ruby's thoughts were scattered by the sound of gunfire. Alarmed, he turned in the saddle to look back. By now he was well up a hill trail, and heat-haze on the plain below made it difficult to get a clear view of the house. He took from his saddle-bag a spy-glass which he had used to good purpose in the closing days of the war to not fight and waste life any more for a cause that was lost, finding ways around the pockets of Southern resistance and Yankee aggression to escort the ragged band of men under his command safely back behind Southern lines, where they dispersed and made their way back to their family and homes, if they had families and homes left.

He saw three men, dressed in grubby grey uniforms, wrestling a rifle from Sarah and dragging her towards the cabin; men whose intentions, even at distance, could not be misinterpreted.

One of the men was holding his wounded right arm, no doubt the result of the rifle shot which had alerted Ruby. Spurring his mount forward, his anger as hot as Hell's coals, Frank Ruby galloped back down the hill trail disregarding the perils of the rocky terrain in his desire to reach his sister before the men took the pleasure they so obviously had in mind.

A time or two his tired horse flagged, and the mare would have stumbled headlong had it not been for Ruby's expert horsemanship. On reaching the end of the hill trail, he raced across the flat plain to the cabin. Halfway across, his heart staggered on hearing Sarah's anguished scream. He pushed the mare far beyond the horse's store of stamina, and, as he galloped into the yard, the mare's legs buckled and the horse went down, pitching Ruby forward. The hard, stony ground of the yard came up fast to meet him, and he feared that when he met the ground he'd be in no fit condition to help himself or Sarah.

His left shoulder met the ground hard and the pain drove sweat out through him as it ran along his spine twanging every nerve on it. He felt the sharp stones of the yard's surface tear the skin off his back as he tumbled over and skidded along its surface. A red haze of pain swam in front of his eyes, and he fought off the cloak of darkness drifting down on him.

There was a man in the cabin door brandishing a cocked six-gun, trying to gauge exactly the point where Ruby would become a stationary target.

Ruby battled to get his own six-gun

from his holster, and be ready to get off a shot the second he settled. He knew that all the advantage lay with the man in the cabin door. Just as he slid to a halt, he forced himself to roll aside just in time to avoid the bullet that bit the dust where he had been. That established that the man was an expert gun-handler. Coming out of the roll, fighting every tortured muscle in his body, Frank Ruby came on to his right knee, crouched and fired. The man in the door staggered back, grasping at his chest to try and stop the pulses of blood escaping from his shattered heart. He teetered and then toppled forward.

The second man of the trio broke from the door and threw himself sideways to the ground, just as Ruby's load ripped a chunk of wood from the door. His gun blasted at Ruby, but obviously and thankfully, his skill with a pistol was not as efficient as had been the first shooter's.

The man ran for the cover of a nearby water trough. His mistake. Ruby double-triggered. The man did a funny dance before folding.

He had used four bullets. Had he two left? Ruby could not be sure. And the man still inside the house had not allowed his heart to rule his head, no doubt figuring, and rightly so, that all the advantage would lie with him if Ruby decided to flush him out. And what alternative did he have? Right now, driven by lust, the most powerful of man's desires, he might be raping Sarah, which left no time for Ruby to ponder or plan. His strategy had to be one of directness and therefore foolhardiness.

He rushed the house, trying as best he could to weave and dodge on legs that simply wanted to buckle.

10

Ten feet . . .

Twenty . . .

Still no response from the house. As he had thought, the man's lust had most likely overriden all other considerations. In the war he had seen men driven so before, bedazzled by the insanity of the primal urge that made all other matters, including their own lives, of secondary importance to its completion.

Thirty feet . . .

Phooosshck!

The air around Ruby was shaken by the thunder of a shotgun blast. He knew that he would now be entering the hereafter in a million pieces had Sarah not clawed the man's face. The man had used both barrels of the shotgun. Ruby noted that the man was not wearing a gunbelt, but he was wearing a sheathed knife which could be used to harm Sarah or hold her hostage. Sarah, still furiously clawing at her tormentor, rendered Ruby's gun useless. He could not risk hitting her.

He sprinted to the cabin, crashing through the door in a loping stride that took the man with him over the table. Ruby was the unluckier of the two. His shoulder crunched against the leg of the wood-burning stove and pain as sharp as a probing needle numbed his left arm. The man, well versed in rough-house fighting, slipped Ruby's grasp and was upright and kicking seconds before Ruby got to his feet. Ruby shuddered under the boot to his ribs, venomously delivered. He bent over and took an uppercut that swung him across the cabin to crash against the far wall. He saw the flash of the knife in the man's hand. Feigning weakness, which did not call for any great acting skills, Ruby gambled on the man's over-confidence.

Striding towards Ruby, he said to

Sarah, 'I'll be with you in a second, honey.'

The man had Ruby's head yanked back and his throat exposed to the knife's blade when Ruby landed a testicle-crunching knee to his groin. Blood rushed to the man's face, threatening to burst every vein in it. Ruby shook off his grogginess, sprang to his feet, spun the man around, grabbed the knife and opened his throat from ear to ear.

Sarah screamed. Ruby shoved the dying man out into the yard and slammed the cabin door shut to save Sarah from witnessing the rigors of his death.

Great heaving sobs shook Sarah. Ruby took her in his arms. She clung fiercely to him. And all the barriers which the war had built up between them crumbled, driftwood washed away in Sarah's tears. Ruby continued to hold and console Sarah as storm clouds rolled in to darken the evening, shutting out the sun and replacing its brightness with a dark sombreness befitting the evil which had been visited on them.

'Remember how you used to comfort me in a storm, Frank?' Sarah said, quietly.

He recalled. Smiling, he said, 'Only doing what any brother should do for his baby sister.'

Sarah slept. Frank Ruby went to sit in the open door to watch the storm build relentlessly, watching the lightning illuminate the premature twilight, his melancholy mind filled with the memories of times past.

★ ★ ★

In Watts Ridge, Ned Ryan was watching the storm also through the narrow confines of the law-office window. But his preoccupation with the storm was not as studied as was Frank Ruby's. His attention was divided between it and the pair of riders hitching their horses to the saloon hitch rail. The men could have been ranch hands or innocent travellers, but Ryan's instincts told him different. On a casual inspection they looked no different to other men going about their business, getting indoors before the full fury of the storm was unleashed. But Ryan, being a trained observer of visitors to town, saw in their gait the whisper of menace that set them apart.

Their thonged guns were worn with the familiarity of guns often used, hugging their hips with the easy comfort of sidearms that were as natural to the men as the hips they adorned. Their carefully casual glances too, were, in Ryan's assessment, pointers to their profession. They seemed to be looking at nothing, but saw everything. These men, the marshal concluded, were professional killers, not gunfighters; there was a difference. Professional gunfighters killed only by contract or when challenged. No, these men were the worst kind of killers. Men addicted to the drug of murder, who killed simply for the sheer pleasure of watching another man die. And in Ned Ryan's long experience, such men were the most dangerous and deadly of the species.

The marshal swallowed hard, finding that his mouth had dried of spittle. He had seen off many such men in his time as a lawman, but he had been younger then and had not had the impediments of fear and age to deal with. His hands and eyes had been faster then too. Now, though his hands had only slowed a little due to a touch of rheumatism, his eyes had become cloudy and close up images had become less well defined. He would have retired, had the town the resources to pay him a pension. But the war had drained everyone's coffers, and it would take time for them to be replenished. When he had raised the matter of his retirement with the town council only the previous week, their response had been starkly unresponsive.

'Maybe in a year or two, Ned,' the

council chairman had said.

He had agreed. He had no choice. He had told himself that two years was not too long. But now, looking at the two men entering the saloon, Ned Ryan was none too sure. With men like these in town, another day, heck, another couple of minutes might be way too long.

★ ★ ★

Sitting, watching the lightning dance a jig across the yard, Frank Ruby wondered about what the future might hold. Up to a short while ago, he had not had any hopes. However, now that Sarah and he had mended bridges, maybe he would settle down on the farm with her. His grin was rueful, maybe even embrace the Union? But he reckoned that that would take time. He was not a bitter man, he had fought as best he could, and was done with fighting, but he was a proud man, and it was pride which would make the acceptance of the demise of the Confederacy such a bitter pill to swallow.

He heard Sarah stir and hurried to her. Waking, she smiled up at him.

'It's good that you've come, Frank,' she murmured.

11

When morning came, against Sarah's wishes, Frank Ruby tied the men's bodies to their horses and set out for Watts Ridge. Naturally, her nerves were raw after her experience of the day before. However, she knew that the death of the men would need to be reported to the law, and the nearest law was in Watts Ridge, in the person of Ned Ryan.

'I won't delay, Sarah,' he told his sister. 'I'll deliver these curs' bodies to Marshal Ryan and head right back. Meanwhile, it might be a good idea for you to stay with a neighbour. Any along the way, you'd care to stop over with?'

'Well, there's Amy and Sam Delaney, I suppose.'

'Good. I should be back by late evening.'

An hour later as he left Sarah at the

Delaney homestead, where welcome had been fulsome, Sarah fretted.

'You will come back, won't you, Frank?'

'Surely will, Sis,' he reassured her.

'You take care. This is wild country, Frank. Lots of unsettled folk.' She hugged herself, the fear of the previous day's terror still stark in her eyes. 'Some crazy as loons.'

'I'll take care,' he promised her.

'You see,' she said, her mood falsely bright, 'we have so much to talk about, and so much to get done. I've been looking for a strong back like yours for a long time.'

'Now you've got it. Strong and willing, Sarah,' Ruby said, riding away, his grim cargo trailing behind him, each horse tied to the next.

'You tell Ned that I send my best wishes, won't you?' she called after him.

Frank Ruby grinned. 'He'll be glad to hear that, Sarah. I think the marshal's soft on you.'

Sarah, flustered, said, 'Oh, phooey,

Frank! That's silly talk.'

Amy and Sam Delaney exchanged knowing glances, confirming Ruby's assessment of Ned Ryan's fondness for Sarah.

★ ★ ★

The Watts Ridge marshal came from a fitful sleep, his eyes grainy. He had bunked down on the couch in his office instead of going home to the clap-board house at the end of Main which went with the badge-toter's job. The couch was a little short for his long frame, but he had, over the year since his wife had died, spent as much time on it as he had in his feather bed. Ethel and he had not ever been really close. Their marriage having been one of mutual convenience arranged by an Irish matchmaker than one of love, had not had enough substance in it to see them through the trials and tribulations of the hard life of Western living. The coming of the war had made that life harder still, and the end of the war had again brought more trouble in the form of drifting hard-cases and evil trouble-stirrers who had got the lust for killing during the war.

He had not always worn a badge. Ethel, coming from farming stock, had urged him to become a farmer. But he had no love of the land and in turn it had rejected him. Crop failure and earth as often as dry as a hundred-year-old bone for long spells, was their undoing. They had moved to town, where he had taken the marshal's job because no one else wanted to take the risks that went with a badge in times when a lawman could not count on time beyond the immediate second he was living in.

Having failed as a farmer, which was the criteria by which Ethel judged a man, and being positively adverse to being a townie, their marriage had become more fraught. When a chill had turned to fever and Ethel had died, Ned thought that it had been probably her happiest moment in a long time. A religious woman, Ethel Ryan had little doubt that the coming life would be a great improvement on her present one. Ryan figured that his present life, too, would be better without the constant strife which the ill-matched pair were locked into. It was not a matter of blame. It was more a matter of shame that neither, in their disappointment, could find it in their heart to see in the other any redeeming feature.

However, to Ned Ryan's amazement, he missed Ethel more than he could ever have imagined he would. And now spent his days regretting that, too late, he had learned how much she had really meant to him. He now wished that she was waiting for him when he opened the front door of the house, even to argue with him. Maybe, he often pondered, that if there was a life hereafter, the next time round he and Ethel might get it right. Whatever the hell 'right' was between a man and a woman.

Recalling his reason for this particular jaunt on the law-office couch, Ryan got up and went to the window to look along the street to the saloon. The horses of the two riders who had caught his interest the evening before were still hitched to the rail outside the saloon, looking sorrowful, tired and hungry. The marshal's anger was immediate and intense.

'No man should treat his horse in that fashion!' he grumbled.

His anger quickly turned to worry. He had hoped that the men would have ridden on. They were trouble, of that he was certain, and he was also sure that their appearance in his neck of the woods was not accidental.

The marshal's mind turned to the bank. Cash for the setting up of a new mining operation in the hills south of town was in the bank safe, awaiting collection the following day. Not many people knew that it was there, having been delivered to the bank disguised as freight, stores for the bank's business.

He had had his reservations about the notion that the less attention, the less likelihood of trouble there would be, preferring armed guards as a deterrent to any would-be bank robbers.

'If no one knows it's there, Ned,' the bank president had reasoned, when Ryan had raised his doubts with him, 'then no one will steal it. Armed guards would simply focus attention.'

At the time Andrew Long's argument had made sense, he supposed. But now Ryan was not so sure. Maybe, he thought, he should have put his counter argument more forcefully.

'If more than one person knows, it's not a secret any longer,' had been his contention.

Long had been dismissive. 'Only those who can be trusted are in the know. Besides,' — he pointed to a lever on the side of the safe, 'that box is a real tricky item for those uneducated in its ways, Ned.'

Now Ryan wondered if someone had, as Long had put it, gabbed. If getting their hands on the mine's cash was the purpose of the strangers' visit, it could be that they were in town to plan their escape after the heist. The larger outlaw gangs, such as the Yancey Clark outfit, always sent agents ahead. Too many robberies failed when bad planning, like suddenly facing blasting guns or riding into a dead-end street, let them down.

Ned Ryan's dilemma was, should he alert the citizens to try and organize resistance? That might be counter productive and send folk into a flap. Or would it be best to bide his time? Watch the antics of the strangers. Maybe he'd be pleasantly surprised and find that he had read them wrongly. But if he had not . . . Both strategies were risky. The first held the possibility of chaos; the second could leave him as the only man facing the outlaws.

He saw the men come from the saloon and, acting on impulse, grabbed his hat and left the office. The men were in no hurry. Jaded from a night of excess, they sought a couple of chairs on the saloon porch on which to gather their wits.

'Howdy, fellas,' Ryan greeted pleasantly. The men looked up at the marshal with eyes that were still clouded with sleep, liquor and other pleasures. 'Rough night, huh?'

'Pretty rough . . . ' The blond-haired man with intense blue eyes as cold as chips of ice, looked up from his half-stooped position. 'Marshal.'

On hearing his partner's mode of address the second man, shorter but with a mouth that hinted at the meaness inside him, became instantly alert. His smile was nothing more than a bunching of his facial muscles.

'Nice town you've got here, Marshal,' he said. He chuckled and rubbed his groin. 'Friendly, too. Ain't that so, Hank?'

Hank, whose real name was Bowie Quail (a name any lawman worth his salt would have recognized instantly), wanted in most territories for his foul crimes, joined in his partner's laughter

101

which Ryan felt was directed at him.

'Real friendly, Marshal.'

It pained Ryan to know that not so long ago, he would have hauled the men to their feet and had them in their saddles and on their way in a blink. He could not pinpoint when he had lost a good measure of his courage, but he had. Right now he was ready to back off and slink back to the law office. And, with instincts as sharp as any wild animal, Bowie Quail and his partner, the equally vicious Jack Smithers, sensed that fear.

Both killers belonged to the murderous Yancey Clark gang.

'Can me and Louie (Jack Smithers' fake handle) do something for you, Marshal?' Quail asked.

'I was just wondering if you fellas are planning on staying around for long.'

'What d'ya reckon, Hank?' Smithers asked Quail.

'Movin' on right after breakfast, Marshal,' was Quail's reply. 'Of course, we'll be visiting, now that we'll be punching cows for Rupe Morgan.'

The lie was slickly and convincingly delivered. Quail complimented himself on having done his homework in finding out the kind of detail that now added legitimacy to his lie, once the need to lie had become necessary.

Relieved, Ryan said, 'You boys'll be working for the Morgan ranch?'

'Yes, sir. It's as Hank says, Marshal,' Smithers confirmed.

'Rupe Morgan's a good man to work for,' Ryan opined.

'That's what we heard. That's why we're here,' said Bowie Quail, alias Hank.

Chuckling, Ryan said, 'He'll work you boys to a standstill. Rupe believes in a return and more for his dollar. Best of luck.'

'Why, thank you kindly, Marshal,' Quail intoned. 'Guess we'll be seeing a great deal of each other now that Louie and me'll be in these parts.'

'I hope that it won't be in an official capacity,' Smithers joked.

'Obey the law, and we'll get along just fine,' Ned Ryan said.

'And that's what we just aim to do, Marshal,' Quail assured Ryan.

'Be seeing you boys around.'

Marshal Ryan headed back to the law office a much relieved man. Not a fool, but being foolish, he was ready to accept the strangers' word, rather than applying the caution he would have not so long ago. And he ignored the fact that, had the men been the cow punchers they claimed to be, the last thing they would have done was mistreat their horses the way they had. Wranglers and horses had a mutual dependency, and therefore a mutual respect. And no ranch hand would let his horse suffer the elements. In fact, its needs would take precedence over their own.

★ ★ ★

Frank Ruby sensed a presence before it materialized. When it did, he stopped dead in his tracks. Not that he had much choice, because the riders who had come from the trees on the trail ahead were blocking it. However, the main reason for his abrupt yank on the reins was his recognition of the man leading the group.

Yancey Clark.

'Well, hello there, Frank,' the man cheerfully greeted Ruby. 'It's been a long time.'

'Not long enough,' Ruby flung back.

Yancey Clark looked beyond Ruby to the bodies draped over their horses.

'That's a pretty ugly cargo you've got in tow, Frank,' he observed.

'That it is. It's a hot day and it's beginning to smell. So if you fellas would —'

'What's your hurry, Frank?' Clark said, his lips smiling but his eyes glittering with evil intent. 'Me and the boys were just about to grub. You're welcome to join us.'

'No, thanks.'

'That's mighty unfriendly, Frank,'

Clark sighed. 'Where have your Dixie manners got to?'

Ruby made to ride on, but the men closed ranks.

'My guess is that you're headed for Watts Ridge,' the gang-leader speculated. 'You were always a lawabiding cuss and you'll want to do things right by the law, by informing the marshal of the killings.'

Yancey Clark sighed wearily.

'Why don't you rest awhile with us, Frank?' he said. 'You see, pretty soon, Watts Ridge is going to have a lot of lead in the air.' He chuckled. 'Unhealthy, that.' He turned to the man on his right. 'Harry, why don't you escort my friend Frank to our present . . . shall we say, address.'

The men joined in Yancey Clark's mocking laughter.

Frank Ruby cursed his luck. Meeting Yancey Clark on the road was akin to meeting Satan himself.

12

The trail they followed was a winding and narrow one, leading up into the hills south of Watts Ridge to a canyon which turned out to be an unexpectedly fertile oasis in the otherwise barren terrain. It was a good perch for any man who needed to survey the countryside and trails leading to Watts Ridge. From the canyon's high reaches, nothing would be missed. Frank Ruby reckoned that it was an interest in Watts Ridge and its comings and goings which was the purpose of Yancey Clark making camp in the canyon.

During the ride there, Clark had not spoken. In fact no man had said a single word. Dismounting at the camp, Ruby broke the silence.

'What's this all about, Yancey?' he asked the outlaw, whose blood-soaked deeds had, during the closing stages of the war and after the war, become notorious, putting his face on Wanted posters in several territories. The last dodger Ruby had seen had had a price of $10,000 on Yancey Clark's head, dead or alive.

'Isn't it fitting for friends to talk?' Clark answered.

Bluntly, Ruby reminded the outlaw, 'We're not friends, Yancey. In fact we haven't been friends for a long time.'

Clark chuckled. 'Then comrades-in-arms, Frank.'

'That neither.'

Clark's face set in stone. 'Heard that you went along with the South's betrayal.'

'Honourable surrender,' Ruby opined.

He scoffed. 'That a fact. Well, I don't see it that way one little bit. I figure that the South is still at war. And will be until,' he snorted, 'the *honourable surrender* is reversed.'

'The war's over, Yancey,' Frank Ruby stated bluntly. 'It's time to mend bridges and make America the great country it can be. And I don't believe for a minute that your plundering and pillaging has anything to do with reviving the South's fortunes.'

'Talky sort o' fella, ain't he, boss,' Yancey Clark's right-hand man said.

'Always was, Harry,' Clark told his sidekick. 'Frank here never thought that men who did what needed doing to win the war, whatever that might be, was right.' He slapped Ruby on the shoulder. 'A real moral fella, is Frank Ruby.'

Ruby walked to his horse.

'Where're you going, Frank?' Clark asked pleasantly.

'To deliver my cargo to the marshal in town.'

Ruby was in the saddle when he heard a pistol being cocked. He turned. Yancey Clark's gun was on him.

'Now that is not a good idea, Frank,' he said. 'I'd like you to stay as my guest for a spell.'

'Prisoner, you mean,' Ruby grated.

Clark laughed. 'That, too.' He levelled the gun on Ruby. 'Now you just climb down. We've got dead to bury.'

Ruby glanced to the three bodies he had in tow. 'Your men?'

Yancey Clark nodded. 'I was wondering where they had got to. Took off yesterday, all itchy for a woman. You think they found one, Frank?'

'That's why they're dead.'

Clark snorted. 'Sarah? Mighty fine woman, your sister.'

'You knew where they were headed?'

Yancey Clark nodded again. 'Told them boys. You've got to understand, Frank. Women, for men like us who spend long spells in the wilderness, have got to be taken where they're found.'

Frank Ruby's lunge at Clark was cut painfully short by one of the gang's rifle butts between his shoulder blades. He fell in front of Clark, clutching at his back.

'Were you trying to do me harm, Frank?' Yancey Clark asked with sweet disbelief. 'Now what kind of friend does that make you?'

Clark's boot shot out to connect with the side of Ruby's head. Clark massaged his right hip. 'It's that old war wound acting up again,' he chuckled. 'Makes my leg go all queer on me.'

The gang's laughter was a collective guffaw.

'You boys' — two men stepped forward at Clark's beckoning — 'make our guest comfortable.' He leaned down beside Ruby. 'You see, Frank,' he explained, 'we can't just let you ride into town and tell the marshal that we're in the vicinity. That would be foolish, us intending to rob the bank as we are.'

'Lotsa wimmen in town, too,' Harry said, massaging his groin.

'Now, fellas,' Yancey Clark mockingly pleaded, 'they'd be ladies.'

'Ladies,' one of the outlaw's sniggered. 'That mean they don't have what other women's got, Yancey?'

'Oh, they've got what other women have got all right, Bengy.'

In mock puzzlement, much to the

111

snide amusement of his fellow gang members, Bengy said, 'Then if they've got what they've got, and I've got what I've got, what's the problem, Yancey?'

Yancey Clark shrugged. 'No problem at all, Bengy. No problem at all.'

13

Having blinded himself to the gaping holes in Bowie Quail and Jack Smithers' tall yarn, Ned Ryan was resting easy, now that his misgivings had not come back to bite him. The two visitors to town who had given him cause for worry were riding out, though a mite late, it being almost dark.

'See you boys,' he called from the law-office door as they rode past. 'Tell Rupe I said hello.'

'Sure will, Marshal,' Quail said pleasantly.

Watching them into the distance, the marshal murmured, 'You're getting too old for this job, Ned, thinking those fellas were trouble.'

He went back inside, figuring on a nap before he made his way to the town eatery for supper. As he dozed off, he heard the creak of a wagon on the street outside and idly wondered who it might be. However, he did not dwell on the matter and searched for the snug niche on the couch which sometimes was more ellusive than a straying husband. Feeling the curve of the niche on the small of his back, just at exactly the right spot, he hoped that the footsteps on the boardwalk outside the office would go on by. When they changed direction just as they drew level with the window, he knew that his hope was dashed. Ryan cursed silently and sprang off the couch, not wanting anyone to catch him napping on the town's time. He was behind his desk writing an imaginary report when the door opened and Rupe Morgan stepped inside.

Pleased to see an old friend, Ryan's mood lightened.

The rancher looked to the couch and grinned. 'You sure can get off that rig and behind your desk faster than a snake can spit, Ned.'

Ryan thought about protesting, but

Rupe Morgan knew him too well to try and fool him.

'Well,' Ryan growled, 'now that I'm awake what do you want, you cantankerous old buffalo?'

'Nothing.'

'Nothing!'

'Just dropped by to pay my respects. And,' he pulled a bottle of Kentucky Rye from under his coat, 'share a couple of shots.'

Ryan picked up the bottle of rye from the desk, its contents shimmering in the waning sunlight coming through the window to the left of his desk.

'Finest there is,' Rupe Morgan said. 'Brought a couple of glasses, too. Didn't fancy drinking out of your shaving mug, like last time.'

The rancher placed a pair of cut crystal glasses on the desk, into which he poured liberal helpings of the rye. He then took a cigar from his pocket. Ryan, a committed anti-smoker, grimaced. Rupe Morgan smugly bit off the top of the Mexican lung-rotter and spat it out. Smugger still, he struck a match, pulled on the cigar with all the might of his lungs, and let the smoke waft towards the marshal. Half, if not more of the pleasure from the cigar, would be in seeing Ned Ryan's nostrils twitching disapprovingly.

'When are you going to chuck the weed, Rupe?' Ryan asked, genuinely concerned for the rancher's health. 'If the Creator had intended men to smoke, He'd have put a chimney on them.'

'Just 'cause you never puffed, doesn't mean we all have to forego the pleasures of the weed, Ned.'

'Never figured what pleasure a man could get from blowing smoke.' Ryan slugged down a half of the rye and sighed contentedly. 'On the other hand, a good whiskey is God's nectar.'

He studied his old friend.

'You look a tad peaky, Rupe. You drive yourself too hard. You should rest more. You're a crusty old rooster now, not a strutting cock. And you've got a whole passel of old-timers working for you, that you should replace with young bucks.'

Rupe Morgan, a man who knew the value of a dollar and how to hold on to it, hired oldsters because they came cheaper than the kind of young buckaroos the two men who had just ridden out of town were.

'At least the two hands you've now hired are strapping fellas.'

'Hands? Hired?' Rupe Morgan asked, puzzled.

'Yeah. Just left town. In fact, your paths must have crossed.'

'You mean the two fellas suffering the demons after a bender?' the rancher checked.

Ryan grinned. 'That would be an apt description, I guess.'

'Hired them!' the rancher yelped. 'My guess is that they wouldn't know on which end a cow wears her tail!'

'You didn't hire them?'

Ned Ryan's fears came back to haunt him.

'I'm long in the tooth, Ned, not short a straw.'

'Then why did they say that you hired them?'

The rancher shrugged. 'Maybe they meant that they were going to drop by looking for work. Fat chance, I say.'

'Maybe,' the marshal said, doubtfully. 'But I got the impression that you had already given them jobs, Rupe.'

'Nope.' The rancher finished his drink and stood up to leave. At the door he called back, 'I've got some chores to do in town, Ned. I'll be back to finish that bottle later.'

'Yeah,' Ryan said, absent-mindedly. 'Sure, Rupe.'

Preoccupied, the marshal opened a desk drawer full of dodgers, most yellowed and useless now, those wanted, dead or breaking rocks in prison. He had meant to clear out the drawer a hundred times but had never got round to it, seeing it as a chore to be long-fingered if at all possible. Most of the Wanted posters he slung into the waste basket under his desk, until the face on a faded dodger brought him up short. It was the face of the stranger called Hank. Only the name on the dodger read Bowie Quail. Ryan's blood ran cold. A further brief search unearthed a dodger for a gent called Jack Smithers — Louie.

Both Yancey Clark henchmen.

Quail was wanted for every known outrage: rape, murder, bank robbery. Smithers' list of grisly doings, if not Quail's equal, was not trailing far behind. And they rode with the Yancey Clark gang, murderers every one. Their story was that they did not accept the South's capitulation and were still fighting the war. But all that that story was intended to do, was to give some kind of heroic legitimacy to their murderous and barbarous acts of wanton skulduggery, to those foolish enough to believe such drivel, the gullible who still yearned for the South's past to be restored. Yancey Clark and his cohorts were nothing more than they had been towards the end of the war, murdering scum, not fighting under a flag, or for any cause other than their own greedy ends.

'Interesting picture, ain't it, Marshal?'

Only a second before, Ryan had felt the cold draught on his back when someone had opened the rear door of the jail. He swung around in his chair to face a gloating Bowie Quail and his equally gloating partner Jack Smithers.

Quail said, ' Jack and me figured we'd best pay a visit when we saw Rupe Morgan call on you. The cat was out of the bag, you see. Lucky that Jack knew Morgan by sight. His old man used to work for him.' He sniggered. 'Until Jack, on a visit to see him, decided to borrow a couple of dozen longhorns.'

'I figured that Morgan owed my pa,' Smithers said. 'Working him and the other old-timers the way he did for half of what he'd have to pay a younger man.'

'You're here to rob the bank, aren't

you?' Ryan asked disconsolately, already knowing the answer to his question.

'Ain't the marshal a smart *hombre*, Jack?' Quail mocked. 'The thing is, now that you've tumbled to who we are and what we're in town for, what do you think I should do about it, Marshal?'

★ ★ ★

Frank Ruby lay staked out on the stony ground. Above him a snake dangled from a piece of rawhide string, wriggling, its glinting eyes on Ruby. Out of range yet to sink its fangs in him, but for how long more? Alongside the sliver of string a lamp burned, its glass globe getting hotter by the second. Soon the bone-dry rawhide string would begin to smoulder and then catch fire. It would burn through and drop the snake riled and spitting on its hapless and helpless victim.

It was a punishment which Yancey Clark had handed out many times before. Often to Yankees, and even more often to men in his own ranks who had in some small way displeased him. And now, as then, his eyes glowed with an evil excitement as he observed the cruel punishment unfold and conclude.

Clark had a way with snakes that no other man had. Ruby had seen the man from Louisiana work his magic before. Somehow, he could look a snake in the eye and hold it mesmerized. And once hypnotized, he could pick up the snake like another man might a cat or a dog and stroke it, communicating with the reptile in a strange whining, that made a man's skin crawl as much as the snake did. After a couple of minutes of this snake-talk, the reptile was Yancey Clark's compliant and willing servant.

'That sure is tough rawhide, Yancey,' said one of the gang watching Frank Ruby's ordeal.

'How long more you figure?' another outlaw asked Clark.

'Don't know,' Clark answered. 'That's what makes it all so darn exciting.'

As the lamp's globe became hotter, tendrils of smoke curled from the rawhide string. Picking up on the smoke and sensing fire, the snake began to wriggle furiously, putting more strain on the string.

The tendrils of smoke became puffs.

'Won't be long now, fellas,' Yancey Clark promised, the evil glint in his eyes glowing as fiercely as the snake's.

The string caught fire!

14

Bowie Quail took on a thoughtful pose, as if pondering on an insurmountable problem. 'What dy'a reckon we should do with the marshal, Jack?' he enquired of his partner.

'Kill him,' Smithers said, simply.

Quail's face registered mock horror. 'Kill a lawman.' And turning to Ryan, 'Ain't killing a lawman breaking the law, Marshal?' When Ryan ignored his taunt, he grabbed him by the throat and growled, 'Well, ain't it?'

'Yes,' the marshal croaked, his voice constricted by Quail's vice-like grip on his windpipe.

'Then we can't do that, Jack. We've got to respect the law.'

Smithers sniggered. 'Ain't you got all righteous of a sudden, Bowie.'

'Besides,' Quail went on, 'I figure that a dead marshal would be a liability.'

'How d'ya figure that?' Smithers asked.

''Cause citizens will be dropping by to see the marshal, and if he ain't here . . . Well, they'll be asking why he ain't. Rupe Morgan is calling back for one. So we've got to keep the marshal alive to meet his guest, don't we?'

Jack Smithers shrugged. 'We could kill the marshal and just bust that rancher's skull when he walks in.'

'If we did that to every caller, we'd have more bodies than a damn mortuary!' Quail snapped. 'No, we've got to ask the marshal to help us to make everything look normal. You'll do that, Marshal, won't you?'

Ned Ryan hated the way he readily nodded his agreement. Of late, as the years piled on, he had found that facing up to hardcases had become more and more difficult. He fooled himself that age played a part in his back-sliding, because he did not want to admit to fear or cowardice. And he knew that pretty soon, if he did not halt his slide, he'd be running away instead of just backing off.

'See, Jack,' Quail said. 'The marshal understands that no one must notice anything different. 'So, Marshal,' he instructed Ryan, 'nothing will be. Every time any one steps through that door, I'll be watching. One hint of trouble from you and I'll kill you and your visitor. Understood?'

'Understood,' Ryan said, breathlessly.

'Me and Jack won't bother you for long. Come morning, Yancey Clark and the boys will be riding in to heist the bank.

'You do as you're told and you'll still be sucking air when we leave. Step out of line and . . . ' Quail left the threat hanging in mid-air. He fired up a Mexican cheroot and contentedly puffed on the foul-smelling weed. A man at ease, because he was a man in control.

★ ★ ★

The outlaws watched Frank Ruby's terror as the rawhide string holding the snake burned through, wondering like Ruby himself was, when the weight of the snake would snap the string. Wriggling furiously as it was, alarmed by the fire at its tail, it would only be seconds.

Ruby was in a lather of sweat. The snake was getting more and more agitated. The string quivered. The snake dropped lower, almost within striking distance. Its fangs curled towards Ruby and were only inches short of his face. The snake now dangled on a sliver of rawhide; the sliver vanished a second later.

The snake was falling. Ruby tensed and waited for the deadly fangs to puncture his flesh. Suddenly the snake's head exploded. Ruby was only vaguely aware of the gunfire. The snake was tossed in the air by the impact of the bullet, and a second bullet tossed it higher still, before the mangled snake fell dead alongside Ruby.

Yancey Clark holstered his smoking gun.

'Give our guest some grub, Barney,' he ordered the camp cook.

'And after?' Ruby asked.

'You ride into town with us tomorrow and hold up the bank. And after that you won't be left with much choice but to ride with us.'

'Never!'

'You'll think differently when you're a bank robber. You'll be marked as a Yancey Clark man. It'll be ride with us or face the law or a bounty hunter on your own.'

'And I thought you were doing me a favour by saving my life,' Frank Ruby said, with a sombre anger.

★ ★ ★

Ned Ryan tensed as he heard boots on the boardwalk.

'Looks like we've got company, Marshal,' Bowie Quail said. He thought about stubbing out the cheroot he was smoking, but changed his mind and placed it on the edge of Ryan's desk. 'No point in wasting a good smoke.'

He vanished through the door leading to the cells on Smithers' tail, a split second before the door of the law office opened and Rupe Morgan stepped inside. But not before warning Ryan about the inadvisability of hinting that there was anything wrong.

'Howdy, Rupe,' Ryan greeted in a stiffish manner. 'Business down?'

'Yeah. Doesn't take long for folk to take your money.'

'You'll be getting back to the ranch without further delay then,' Ryan said, rising from his chair to turn Morgan round.

Puzzled, the rancher shook him off. 'Not before I have another shot of that rye.'

The marshal chuckled. 'Dang. I thought you'd have forgotten that by now, and the bottle would be all mine.'

Ryan grabbed the rancher's arm and ushered him towards the door.

'Are you OK, Ned?' the rancher asked, more concerned than annoyed.

'Sure I'm OK.'

'You ain't acting OK. It ain't your way to be so unfriendly.'

'Sometimes all a man needs is his own company, Rupe.'

'Shucks!' the rancher exclaimed. 'You're kicking me out?'

'I'll ride out your way in a day or two. We can finish that bottle then.'

Rupe Morgan snorted. 'Keep the damn bottle. It ain't worth sharing with a fella who only wants his own company.'

'I've got a whole pile of paperwork to do,' the marshal said, and then growled, 'And with folk dropping by all the time out of the blue, I'll never get it done.'

Morgan stiffened. 'Didn't know that I was such a nuisance, Ned. So I'll get out of your hair.'

'Good,' Ryan said, curtly. 'Maybe next time you're in town — '

'I'll seek out more congenial company,' Morgan interjected waspishly.

'You do that,' Ryan told his old friend.

The rancher was at the door when he paused and turned.

'What now?' Ryan asked brusquely.

The marshal quaked when he saw Rupe Morgan glance beyond him to the smouldering cheroot which Bowie Quail had left behind. Knowing Ryan's aversion to the weed, the rancher was quick to work out that the marshal had another guest — one whom he did not want him to see. Or one who did not want to be seen. And there was a world of difference.

The glance exchanged between Rupe Morgan and Ned Ryan spoke more than a million words. Morgan's glance went to the partially closed door leading to the cells, the only place where Ryan's unwelcome guest or guests could be hiding.

'Well, I guess with you in this polecat mood, I'll be moseying along now,' the rancher said, grumpily.

But as he turned to leave, a knife was

lodged between his shoulder blades by Quail. When the rancher spun around clutching at the knife, the second knife which Quail carried was despatched to Rupe Morgan's throat.

Morgan fell to his knees, gagging. His breath came in short gasps until he shuddered and stopped breathing all together.

Though shocked by the death of his old friend, Ryan took advantage of the catastrophe to slide his hand under the desk to where he had a six-gun secreted, a fall-back weapon that had served him well in the past, but not this time. Jack Smithers, as alert as a rattler, clipped the marshal with his pistol knocking him off his chair to the floor. He followed through with a boot to the ribcage that had vomit spewing from the marshal's mouth. Ryan curled up and groaned.

'Want me to kill him?' Smithers asked Quail, eager to render the service.

'Don't be dumb!' Quail rebuked his partner. 'Get the marshal back in his chair. Then go make some coffee.'

'We don't have to pamper no lawman,' Smithers argued. 'We don't need Yancey Clark neither. We could take this town by ourselves. They'd run scared.'

Bowie Quail snorted. 'Rode into a small noconsequence town once in Montana when I was riding with the Will Benteen outfit. Will figured like you, Jack. We rode out six men short and with buckshot in our asses.

'We do exactly what Yancey ordered us to do. We sit tight, keep our eyes and ears open, and wait until he shows. Now stop sassing me and make the damn coffee.'

Grumbling, Smithers did as ordered, but Quail kept a keen eye on his partner because he knew well his preference for acting when a man had his back turned. Settled in his chair but hurting badly, Bowie Quail told Ryan, 'Stop your damn whining. You're lucky to be still sucking air.' When Smithers came back bearing a pot of piping hot coffee, Quail poured and laced it with a liberal helping of the Kentucky rye which Rupe Morgan had returned to the law office to finish off. 'Get that inside. It'll ease your hurting.'

Quail froze as footsteps sounded on the boardwalk. The visitor had left the dusty street to step on to the boardwalk. Had he approached along the plank walk-way he would have given warning of his imminent arrival. If it was a visitor to see the marshal, all hell would break loose because there was no time to have Ryan fully restored. And unless the visitor was coming with a blind-man's cane, he could not fail to see the prone figure of Rupe Morgan the second he opened the door. There wasn't even time for him to get behind the door and slit the visitor's throat as he entered. That meant that he'd have to use his gun, or the caller would flee into the darkness to alert the town. However, using his gun would have the same effect.

'Some damn choice,' he swore angrily.

The law office was well stocked with guns and ammo, and being ace marksmen, he and Smithers could hold out for quite a spell, but the element of surprise for which Yancey Clark had planned would be lost. And, more importantly, the surprise he had planned himself, should a certain gent of his acquaintance join in a scheme he had suggested to him the night before, would be lost too.

Holding the marshal hostage had never been part of the plan. It was a downright stroke of bad luck that the yarn he had spun about hiring out to Rupe Morgan had been rumbled so soon. Now chances were that when Yancey Clark showed up and saw that the town was up in arms, he'd hightail it and leave him and Smithers to be lynched. He knew well how Yancey Clark would figure. There would be other towns and other banks, so why risk being wiped out? Clark had been finding it difficult to recruit men to replace the ones who had been gunned down, because there were too many lawmen and bounty hunters eager to cash in on the price on Clark and his comrade's heads.

The footsteps came straight to the marshal's door.

15

Frank Ruby's thoughts were frantic ones as he searched for a way out of his dilemma. His stock was as low as it could be in Watts Ridge, and when he rode in as part of the Yancey Clark outfit it would seem that all the hatred piled on him would have been justified. A day ago he would not have worried about opinion in Watts Ridge, but now that he had decided to remain on with Sarah to farm, the opinion and goodwill of the townsfolk would be all important. Sarah had been accepted into their midst, but that would change quickly when her brother was part of the Yancey Clark gang. If he did not find some way out of his predicament, Sarah's as well as his future in Watts Ridge would be ruined.

There had been times when the list of Yancey Clark's atrocities had mounted that he had regretted saving his life, but never more so than right now.

Ruby's mind went back to a balmy fall afternoon in Atlanta. As he passed by, Yancey Clark was leaving the residence of a general whose daughter he was courting, not as a prospective wife, but rather as a means to an end. The general was influential — admired by Robert E. Lee himself, it was said. A soldier, one of the legion of men whom Clark had needlessly sacrificed in his quest for rapid promotion, faced him in a cripple's chair, a shotgun primed. Quick to react, Ruby had tackled the invalid soldier, saving Clark's life. Now Yancey Clark's prisoner, he could see the cruel irony of his action that day. Later he would earn Clark's undying hatred by giving evidence at his court martial.

Ruby glanced to his right as he heard the sleepy snort of the man who had been ordered to take the first watch. The man's head was going down. Soon he would be asleep, but the outlaw's slide into slumber would not hand him any advantage, bound hand and foot as he was. He needed free hands and feet if he were to have any chance of changing the bad luck which had dogged him. He could have taken the other trail to town which Sarah's host had pointed out.

'Longer, but safer,' Sarah's neighbour had said.

Fool that he was he had ignored good advice, and had opted for the shorter but more risky route to Watts Ridge and had run smack into Yancey Clark. A lesson for the future had been learned, but it was of little use, seeing that his chances of having a future were pretty slim.

The man on watch tilted sideways. Frank Ruby's eye caught the glint of firelight on the blade of a hunting knife tucked inside the waistband of his trousers.

Now if he had that knife . . .

Bowie Quail dropped his hand to his gun, held his breath and stood as still as a statue.

'No need for more killing,' Ned Ryan croaked, already out of his chair and on his way to the door, his feet dragging. 'I'll get rid of whoever it is.'

'Don't do anything stupid, Marshal,' Quail cautioned.

Bracing himself, Ryan opened the door, smiling broadly.

'Burt. How's Ellie? Heard she wasn't feeling so good.'

Burt said, 'Bronchitis. Ain't easy to shake off.'

'Be sure to tell her I said hello.'

A sudden bout of coughing beset the marshal.

'You don't sound or look so good yourself, Ned,' Burt observed, concerned. 'Guess I'd best help you back inside out of the night air.'

Bowie Quail, who had begun to relax, tensed again.

'Oh, just a chill, Burt. Ain't nothing to fret about.'

'You sure?'

'Sure,' Ryan confirmed.

'Well . . . best be getting on home, I guess. I was only dropping by for a chinwag anyway.'

'Ellie will be expecting you.'

'I guess,' Burt said wearily. 'Her ma had bronchitis. Reckoned I should have known that Ellie would have it too. Weak chests are passed on, you know,' he warned Ned Ryan, 'if you're ever thinking of taking a wife again, Ned.'

'I'll keep that in mind,' Ryan said, gently closing the door. ' 'Night, Burt.'

Ryan sagged against the door, as weak as a day-old kitten. Quail helped him back to his chair.

'You did OK, Marshal,' he complimented. 'Pretty soon now this town will be asleep, and our problems will be over.'

'I think I have a couple of busted ribs,' Ryan groaned.

'I intended you to have,' Smithers chuckled.

'I've got to see the doc.'

Quail shook his head, and stated uncompromisingly, 'No sawbones. You'll just have to take your chances, Marshal.'

★　★　★

Frank Ruby's eyes swept the outlaw camp. Most of the men were deep in a liquor-induced sleep and would probably not hear Gabriel's horn, should he blow it. But there were a few who had not imbibed heavily, Yancey Clark being one, and they might very well hear the slightest rustle of movement attuned as they were to sleeping with one eye and both ears open. There would be a great risk in trying to relieve the man on watch of his knife, but Ruby knew that he had no choice if he wanted to grab his life back from Yancey Clark's evil clutches. And he was not going to throw away his chance of leading the life of a normal man as a farmer, and getting to know his sister Sarah all over again.

He shifted his position a couple of inches and waited for any response.

★ ★ ★

Bowie Quail checked the law-office clock; almost midnight. He had hauled Rupe Morgan's body to one of the cells, and he had dimmed the lamp to discourage callers. Ned Ryan was still sitting in his chair, but looking closer to passing out by the second, maybe even dying. The street was full of the noise of the saloon emptying. Quail hoped that the boisterous humour of the drinkers would not sour as was often the case on the flimsiest whim and ructions would break out which would need the intervention of the marshal who, when he would not put in an appearance voluntarily, would be sought out.

★ ★ ★

Seconds ticked by. Ruby still waited. The man on watch had not moved a muscle. A man turned in his sleep. Mumbling a woman's name, he curled up contentedly. He shifted another couple of inches. Waited again. Nothing. And on he went, tediously closing the gap between him and the man on watch.

Ruby wondered how deep into sleep he was? A dark and disturbing thought haunted him. What if the man was playing possum? Leading him on. Enjoying every second, waiting to spring into action just when his hope was at its highest.

Another couple of inches. A pebble, disturbed by his right boot, rolled down the incline he was on. Ruby gulped. The pebble was rolling straight for a tin cup. If it struck it, it would, he was sure, be louder than a roll of thunder trapped inside a bucket. He willed it to change direction. The pebble wobbled. Almost stopped dead. And then lurched forward again. It glanced off another pebble and took it with it.

Now there were two pebbles rolling towards the tin cup.

* * *

Ned Ryan finally passed out. It was almost one o'clock. Watts Ridge was as still as the inside of a tomb.

'How 'bout some shuteye, Bowie?' Smithers suggested.

'No turning in,' Quail barked.

'What's the point in not gettin' sleep?' Smithers groused. 'Nothin's goin' to happen now.'

'You watch the marshal,' Quail ordered.

'Where're you headed?'

'Checking out the town.'

Jack Smithers shook his head and snorted. 'You got rocks in your head, Bowie, ya know that, don't ya.'

Quail quenched the lamp before opening the door.

'Better to have rocks in your head than bullets in your gut, Jack,' he said, before slipping out into the moonlit night.

★   ★   ★

Frank Ruby watched the pebbles divide and roll separate ways, going either side of the tin cup. For the first time, he began to think that his luck had changed.

16

Ruby edged ever closer to the sleeping man until he was within reaching distance of the knife. The outlaw appeared to have gone into a deep sleep, tilted against a tree. Now came the trickiest part. With his hands tied behind his back, Ruby would have to grope blindly for the knife. He concentrated and fixed the position of the knife in his mind before backing up as close to the man as he dared. The rawhide binding on his wrists would not permit much movement and hinder his dexterity. Also, the tight bond had affected his circulation, and his hands were numb and clumsy. He flexed his fingers to get as much feeling in them as he could. Then he reached for the knife, hoping that his touch would be as feather-light as it needed to be. His fingers felt the cold of the knife.

'Francine,' the man who was dreaming, groaned.

Ruby froze.

'Gawddam, Larry,' the man sleeping alongside him rebuked. 'I ain't Francine. And if I was, you'd be sure surprised to find what you're findin' right now.'

There was a general muttering of complaint before the camp settled down again, with a couple of chuckles thrown in. The man on watch shifted, but did not wake up. Ruby let some minutes go by to let the man settle before again touching the knife. He curled his finger round the handle and gently tested its hold. There was some yield in the knife, but not much. And every shaving of an inch it moved from now on, would carry a heart-stopping risk.

Ruby tried to swallow, but he did not have enough spittle. The knife began to slide. But it was a long way from being free.

★ ★ ★

Bowie Quail, a cautious man, and a man on a mission, hugged the shadows of the town's main drag. He waited until the last of the stragglers from the saloon dispersed before he left the shadowed door of the general store and crossed the street. He paused, his eyes scanning the street, before he slipped into the alley that ran between a dress-maker's shop and the bank. Once in the alley, Quail hurried along to the rear of the bank, his excitement mounting now that he was about to implement the plan that had come to mind full-blown the previous night on crossing paths with a friend who possessed a very special talent for opening locks — all sorts and kinds of locks. Including safe locks. With this gent, one Billy Bob Hall, there were no loud bangs. His work was silent and swift. Just what was needed to rob a bank in a sleeping town, and be long gone before Yancey Clark showed up.

Later the previous night, when Smithers was out cold from liquor and exhaustion, Quail had paid Billy Bob a visit in his room at the saloon, and had told him of the riches that would be in the town bank the following night.

'Don't you ride with the Yancey Clark outfit, Bowie?' Hall had asked, worried about the danger of crossing that particular gent.

'Sure do,' Quail had readily admitted, seeing no point in lying. And added that the riches in the bank safe were the object of Clark's attention.

Hall, not the bravest of honchos, squirmed.

'Don't sound such a good idea to me, Bowie, to heist what Yancey Clark's got his eye on.'

Billy Bob had good reason to worry. Yancey Clark skinned men alive for looking crooked at him. For robbing him of a fortune, Lord knew what punishment he'd dream up. One thing was certain, if caught, it would be terrible and Satanic.

It had taken Bowie Quail a lot of breath to persuade Hall that the gain outweighed the risk.

'What about Smithers?' Hall had worried.

'You let me take care of Jack, Billy Bob,' Quail had said.

Quail had planned simply to slit Jack Smithers' throat when the time came. But when the marshal had eyed them suspiciously, and he had to spin Ryan the tall tale about working for Rupe Morgan, his plan for Smithers' demise went awry. They had to leave town to back up his lie. Then they had to return to town pronto to make sure that the lie was not revealed to the marshal, which would have reawakened his suspicions about them. But, fortuitously, the twists and turns had worked out well. Had he killed Smithers he would have been forced to stand guard over the marshal, and could not have set his plan to rob the bank in motion.

Billy Bob Hall stepped from the shadows to greet Bowie Quail.

Ruby felt the hunting knife slide clear of the outlaw's waistband. The man stirred. He waited. Resisting the urge to put as much distance between him and the sleeping man as quickly as possible, Ruby only went a short distance away. At a spot he had already picked out, and working blind, he wedged the handle of the knife as firmly as he could between a set of rocks, and hoped that its hold was firm enough for him to cut through the binding on his wrists.

He began the tedious work of cutting. It was slow, nerve-rattling work. He could not apply any pressure, because with his back to the knife he could not see to judge how firmly secured the knife was. If the knife came loose, it would clatter between the rocks and his hope of escape would be gone.

Steadily, a thread at a time, Frank Ruby felt the binding loosen.

★ ★ ★

Jack Smithers went to the law office window to peer out into the dark nervously. It was a useless exercise. With the moon momentarily hidden, he might as well be looking down an unlit mineshaft. What he was looking for was a glimpse of Bowie Quail.

'How darn long does it take to check out this burg?' he grumbled. Behind him, Ned Ryan stirred and groaned. 'Be quiet!' he grated. 'Or I'll slit your damn throat and be done with it.'

The outlaw returned to his nervous perusal of the town, his worry hiking by the second. He checked the wall clock. Quail had been gone for almost thirty minutes. He began to fret that some mischief might have befallen his partner. Maybe right now, he thought frantically, Quail might be the town's prisoner and its citizens were forming a plan to deal with him.

He decided that he'd give Quail five more minutes. If he wasn't back by then, he'd go looking for him. Or maybe he'd just mount up and ride off while he still had the chance. He cursed the rotten luck that had pitched him and Quail into the predicament they found themselves. They had done what they had come to do. They had sized up the town's mood, and the lie of the land to find the safest route out of town as Yancey Clark had instructed them. Many a dunderhead bank robber had got everything right except his escape route, and had paid the price for his slip-shoddiness.

'If we just hadn't dallied with those saloon doves,' Smithers groaned.

Once approached by the marshal they had been forced to improvise and came up with what seemed a reasonably safe lie. It was downright bad fortune as they rode out of town to have crossed paths with Rupe Morgan.

★ ★ ★

Frank Ruby's hands came free. He massaged his wrists to get the circulation going. Then he quickly cut through the binding on his ankles. He stood, slowly limbering up. His toes tingled as blood reached them. He took a couple of seconds to get full feeling back in his legs. Clumsiness now, and he could be right back to where he had been.

Gingerly watching every step he took, he made his way through the camp to where the horses were. He saddled his horse, still not fully believing his good luck. A second later, as he swung into the saddle, his apprehension was fully justified. He froze on hearing the sound of a pistol being cocked.

'Nice going, Frank,' Yancey Clark said. 'I enjoyed every second of your antics. Step down. Slow and easy.'

The camp was now coming awake.

'Spence,' Clark yelled.

The man whose knife Ruby had used to free himself with came running. 'Sorry, Yancey. Musta dozed off.'

Yancey Clark shot him right between the eyes.

17

Yancey Clark turned his attention back to Frank Ruby, his smile an inadequate prop to mask the fury glinting in his diamond-bright eyes.

'Now what am I to do with you, Frank?' he uttered, in a manner befitting the scolding of a naughty child. 'You just keep on bucking my company and hospitality.'

'You don't have to put up with it, Yancey,' Ruby said. 'I'll shake off the dust of this camp right this second, and be mighty pleased to do so.'

Addressing the gathered outlaws, each man now fearful of incurring Clark's displeasure, he said, 'You see what I mean, boys? This fella just keeps on riling me.'

A runtish, mean-mouthed man to the front of the crowd opined, 'Deserves killin', Yancey.'

The gang waited for Yancey Clark's response to the outlaw's suggestion before they gave their endorsement or condemnation. The man who had spoken out was the exception. No other man had had grit to voice an opinion either way. In speaking out the man had shown in his outspokeness, his Texas roots. Most Texans said exactly what they meant, take it or leave it. And most times in the West, plain speech was appreciated. But with a loco critter like Yancey Clark, plain speech might not be seen as a virtue but rather as an affront, depending on his frame of mind at that moment. The Texan was also a relative newcomer to the outfit, and ignorant of Clark's moods. He did not know that some-times, what a man thought would please the gang-leader might at that particular moment be offensive in some way. To those who had ridden in the Clark gang for a spell, the risk of offering an opinion on anything was a risk too great to ponder. In the Yancey

Clark outfit, if you had a grain of sense in your skull, you simply obeyed orders.

'I'll be glad to oblige,' the man added.

A quiver of tension ran through the outlaws as Yancey Clark considered the Texan, his blank expression giving not the least hint as to his thoughts.

'That a fact, Harker?' Clark drawled. 'Hear that, Frank?' Ruby impassively returned Clark's gaze. The gang-leader turned back to the Texan. 'I'm not too sure that I appreciate your offer, friend,' he said. 'You see, Frank Ruby and me go back a long way.'

Ruby was of a mind to deny any friendship on his part but he held his tongue. He was dealing with a man whose venom was more poisonous than any snake's. Better to work the rift between Clark and his crony.

'Lippy sort of fella, isn't he?' Ruby said. 'Telling the boss his business.'

'Yeah,' Clark said. 'Lippy, as you say, Frank.'

Ruby was hoping that if the Texan had any friends in the outfit, they might take exception to any punishment which Clark might decide to hand out, should it transpire that the gang-leader deemed that Harker had spoken out of turn.

It was a longshot.

Yancey Clark was a wild card, always had been, totally unpredictable and utterly incomprehensible. Two character traits that would have made him a general anyway, had he had the patience to foster them instead of taking the routes of connivance and skulduggery to reach the lofty rank he had craved.

Smug as a fox with a chicken in its jaws, Yancey Clark said, 'I've got an idea, fellas.'

★ ★ ★

'Howdy, Billy Bob,' Bowie Quail greeted the man stepping out of the shadows at the rear of the bank.

'Thought you might have changed your mind.'

Billy Bob Hall was a great deal paler than Quail recalled from their last meeting. Then he had the pallor of prison; now he had the ghostly paleness of fear.

'I did, a million times. And if I had any sense I'd be walking the other way, Bowie. Robbing Yancey Clark ain't the cleverest thing I've ever done.'

'By the time Yancey will get to know, we'll be long gone,' Quail reassured him. 'No fortune was ever made without taking risks, Billy Bob.'

'Long gone, you say?' Hall complained. 'Has the earth enough space to hide in, if Yancey Clark comes looking?'

'A teller, Clark's inside agent, told him that tonight there's all of two hundred thousand dollars in the bank safe.' He paused, and then slung his final piece of bait to bolster the wavering safecracker. 'Split two ways . . .'

Billy Bob Hall licked dry lips. Bowie Quail saw the flash of greed in his eyes, and tempted him further.

'Split two ways?' Hall panted. 'I thought the split was seventy five/ twenty five?'

'We're partners, ain't we?' Quail said, generously. 'And I've been thinking that it's only right and proper that pards should split everything right down the middle.'

'That's mighty generous, Bowie,' Hall opined.

Bowie Quail looped an arm round Billy Bob's shoulder and gave him a good-buddy hug. 'Now, let's get this over with as quickly as we can, Billy Bob.' He chuckled. 'I want my dust settled by the time Yancey Clark rides in to find that the cupboard is bare.'

Boosted by his good fortune, Billy Bob Hall's doubts about the wisdom of what they were about to do, vanished. His plan had been to head to Mexico and maybe a little further on into the South Americas. But now, his fortune doubled in a flash, he had changed his plans. Now he would go to Europe. He could not read, but he had bunked down in the penitentiary with an educated *hombre* who had murdered his wife for whoring behind his back, who had read a book to him about London, England. That's where he would make for. A rich man, he would have no problem in following the career of a gambler in London. Maybe even in one of those fancy gentlemen's clubs that were mentioned in the book.

'Let's go crack that safe, Bowie,' Hall said eagerly.

★   ★   ★

'Idea?' Harker asked.

Yancey Clark was as pleased as a kid at Christmas. 'I figure that the best thing to do would be to let you gents draw on each other.'

'A gunfight!' one of the outlaws yelled delightedly. 'Just what's needed to brighten a dull night, I say.'

Clark's proposal got unstinting approval, even from the Texan, who was obviously sure that out-drawing Frank Ruby would pose no problem for him.

The gang-leader ordered a nearby man, 'Give him your rig, Bert.'

The man gladly handed over his gunbelt.

'This isn't a fair fight, Yancey,' Ruby said. 'I've had my hands bound for several hours now. Blood has been in short supply to my fingers. They're stiff.'

Clark was unconcerned. 'Can't wait round all night, Frank. The men need shuteye. A couple of hours from now we'll be riding for Watts Ridge to rob the bank.'

'Mebbe if I wore a patch over one eye, boss,' the Texan mocked, placing a hand over his right eye, much to the outlaws' amusement.

Yancey Clark, too, saw humour in Harker's antics. When the horsing around was done with, he sternly ordered Ruby, 'Buckle on that gun and let's get this over with, friend.'

Now, Ruby had an idea.

★ ★ ★

Jack Smithers went to the law-office window for the umpteenth time since Bowie Quail had taken his leave to check out the town, his worry getting keener with every passing second. He pulled back suddenly from the window when he saw a couple of men go by. He swallowed hard when he saw them meet up with another man further along the moonlit street. Maybe their business was perfectly innocent, but usually when doors closed for the night in a Western town, they did not open again before sun-up. Maybe, too, Smithers thought, that with the bank safe stacked with money he was looking at a town patrol. However, if that were the case, how come Bowie Quail had slipped their notice? But from past experience, he knew that Quail could sneak up on a ghost to pick his pockets without the ghost ever knowing he had been around. Quail was the most light-footed and slinkiest-moving man he had ever crossed paths with. In the war, he had crossed back and forth across Yankee lines, passing within inches of Union guards, without them ever having the merest hint of his presence.

He went and shook Ned Ryan awake from his fitful slumber.

'Is the town being patrolled tonight, Marshal?' he demanded to know.

Ryan weakly shook his head. 'The bank figured that the less attention, the better.'

'Then what're them three fellas doin' out there in the street at one o'clock in the mornin'?'

Ryan shrugged, and slipped back into a restless sleep.

Smithers considered that Bowie Quail had spotted the men long before he had, and was lying low until he could make it safely back to the law office. That would make sense. But it would also mean that one of them would have to ride out to warn Yancey Clark about potential opposition to him getting his hands on the bank loot. Another thought sneaked into Jack Smithers' mind: maybe, figuring that the town air would be full of hot lead when Clark rode in, Quail had lit out. Bowie Quail was a man who always put his own interests and hide first.

He glanced back at the sleeping marshal, and decided that he would risk leaving Ryan alone while he followed in Quail's footsteps. It could mean big trouble if Ryan woke up and found that he was alone and free to raise a ruckus. But he could not stand the waiting and uncertainty any longer. He was even considering riding out, but the thought of Clark and Quail's retribution should his departure be premature, was an even stronger fear than the fear already curling his gut.

Outside, in the inky dark night, he could hear the men muttering — the way men did when planning covert action. Smithers sought the deepest shadow he could find and waited. When he saw them move towards the bank with the stealth of a mountain cat, it puzzled him. If they were a town patrol, why would they be moving about like thieves in the night? Unless, of course, they were closing in on someone already inside the bank?

But who could that be?

When he thought about it, it could only be one person — Bowie Quail. But what was he doing in the bank?

★ ★ ★

'Idea?' Yancey Clark asked.

'If I win, I ride,' Ruby said. 'Seems fair to me.'

'Ride, huh?' Clark considered. 'Ride where?'

'Back to the farm.'

Yancey Clark was shaking his head. 'You're a real honest fella, Frank, but how do I know that you wouldn't head straight for town to warn the marshal about my plans to rob the bank?'

'Easy. A couple of your men will ride with me to make sure that I don't.

Better than forcing me to ride with you, Yancey.'

'Yeah?'

'Think about it. A real honest fella might get all sorts of notions and get up to all sorts of tricks, when your mind is given over to robbing the bank.'

'I'd kill you,' Clark stated bluntly.

'You could only do that if you were alive yourself, Yancey.'

'Then maybe we should forget this gunfight, and I can kill you myself right now.'

Frank Ruby had feared, but had also anticipated that twist in events.

'You could do that, Yancey, but that would rob you of the chance to destroy me in the slow fashion you plan to — with me on the run, and my life ruined. No, sir, you'd much prefer to have the enjoyment of seeing lawmen and bounty hunters dogging my trail.'

Yancey Clark laughed in his mirthless way. 'You always were a smart *hombre*, Frank. And you're right about me wanting my pleasure to be as prolonged as possible. But tagging along you'd be risky. The gunfight will go ahead,' he concluded.

'And the deal?' Ruby pressed.

'That, too.'

'Then,' Frank Ruby said, wriggling his fingers to ease out the joints, 'I'm ready when you are,' he told the Texan.

* * *

Billy Bob Hall was a man for whom locks posed no problems. Bowie Quail and he were inside the bank in seconds flat, the door lock undamaged.

'Lock it again,' Quail instructed Hall.

'Why?'

'Because if anyone tried the door they'd find it open,' Quail explained.

'And who'd be trying the door at this time of night?'

'Why take the chance and ruin ours, Billy Bob?' was Bowie Quail's reasoning.

'You were always a cautious man, Bowie,' Hall said.

'It's kept me out of jail and my neck out of a lynch rope.'

Hall relocked the door in the same way he had opened it, with a strange-looking piece of metal bearing several notches of different sizes which he had personally fashioned. Quail tested the door to make sure that it was locked.

'Yes, sir. A real cautious man,' Hall observed.

'A careless man is a foolish man,' Quail retorted. Feeling suddenly apprehensive and trusting his instincts which had served him well in the past, he urged the safecracker, 'Let's get to doing what we're here to do, Billy Bob.'

They went behind the teller's counter and into the manager's office where the safe was located. Billy Bob Hall went to examine the safe.

'Well,' Quail quizzed him impatiently, when only a couple of seconds had passed, 'can you open it?'

'As easy as a tin of beans,' Hall boasted.

'Then what're you waiting for?' Quail asked anxiously, as Billy Bob Hall closed his eyes in deep concentration.

'You gotta get in the right mood, Bowie,' the safecracker murmured, reverentially.

'How long is that going to take?' Quail asked, nervously glancing back into the public area of the bank.

He thought he saw a shadow slanting across the window, but he could not be certain. There were a lot of shadows. And his imagination might be playing tricks, too. All he knew was that he had, for the last couple of minutes, been edgier than a bride on her wedding night.

A moment later, Hall said, 'I'm ready to open this box as soon as I get some light.'

'Light!' Quail yelped.

'I gotta be able to see the darn lock, don't I?' Hall groused.

Grumbling, Quail lit a lamp and cupped his hand round the globe to shield its glow as best he could. 'You

171

never said nothing about light, Billy Bob.'

'Hold the damn lamp steady, will ya,' the safe-cracker moaned.

★   ★   ★

'We goin' to wait all night?' Harker griped.

Yancey Clark agreed with the Texan. 'The man's got a point, Frank. Are you going to draw or not?' Frank Ruby stopped massaging his wrists. His fingers were still a little stiff, but it was probably down as much to age as lack of circulation from the tight binding on his wrists.

'I'm ready,' he told Clark. 'You call it.'

Yancey Clark picked up a twig and held it aloft.

'When I drop this, you boys draw.'

★   ★   ★

Jack Smithers hurried across Main to the edge of the alley leading to the rear of the bank. He peered into the alley, just in time to see the three men disappear behind the bank. He stepped carefully into the alley. Curiosity often earned a man a fast bullet in the gut.

★   ★   ★

Bowie Quail waited breathlessly as Billy Bob Hall went to work, teasing and coaxing the safe's lock with the curious-looking tool which Hall claimed matched every known lock mechanism. And had proved as much.

'How long more?' he quizzed the safecracker, tension giving his voice an uncharacteristic squeakiness.

'Just a matter of finding the right notch, Bowie.'

After another fretful minute, when Billy Bob wiped sweat from his brow, Quail challenged him, 'You can't open the damn thing, can you?'

Hall shot the outlaw a worried glance. 'I can open it all right. But . . . '

'But what?'

'Well, I'm getting a bad feeling about this safe, Bowie.'

'Bad feeling? What kind of bad feeling?'

'That it would be best left unopened kind of bad feeling.' He added, 'I get these moods, Bowie. I've come to trust them.'

'To hell with your moods. Open the damn safe!'

Fearful of being on the receiving end of one of Quail's well-known rages, Billy Bob, against his better judgement, turned the safe's lock. Bowie Quail panted with anticipation. Then with a sudden shiver, glanced behind him.

'What is it?' Hall asked edgily.

Unable to pinpoint his anxiety, Quail shrugged. He crept to the edge of the partially open office door and peered out, just as the lock of the bank's rear door was forced open.

Three men entered the bank.

'This is loco. We'll never crack that safe,' the smallish man bringing up the rear complained.

'Oh, stop your moaning, Josh,' the leader of the trio rebuked him. 'All we can do is try.' There was the rattle of keys. 'I've got me every key in the darn West right here. One of them's bound to open that box, I figure.'

'Yeah,' the third man, as close to a beanpole as a man could get, enthused, 'we might just hit the jackpot, Josh.'

They were halfway across the public area of the bank when Bowie Quail's first knife sliced the air. The leading man looked unbelievingly at the knife protruding from his chest, and then looked to his partners for an explanation before crashing to the floor. Bowie's second knife caught the man called Josh in the windpipe. The beanpole's hands reached for the ceiling. Bowie Quail stepped from the manager's office.

'Howdy,' he greeted the shaking man. 'Seems that this bank is busier at night than it is by day.'

'I-I'll leave right now,' the beanpole gasped. 'Won't say a word. Honest.'

'Leave? Aren't you going to have your share? There's plenty.'

'Share?' the beanpole asked, astonished.

'Sure, my friend,' Quail said.

The man's greed momentarily overrode all other factors, including common sense. Straight thinking went out the window. Quail had already killed his partners, so why should he spare him? The couple of seconds lapse in logic had been enough time for Quail to close the gap between them. He rammed his gun deep into the man's gut to muffle the gun's blast.

'Now let's get that money and get out of here,' he ordered Billy Bob Hall.

★   ★   ★

Yancey Clark dropped the twig he was holding aloft.

18

The Texan was fast. Faster than Ruby.
His gunhand had moved in a blur, but
he was not as quick-witted as Ruby.
He stood stock still, gloating, gun
blasting. Whereas Ruby, in the split-
second it had taken him to realize that
he wasn't nearly fast enough, had
dived aside. While falling he triggered
his six-gun. Harker staggered back
clutching his chest, looking in disbelief
at the blood seeping through his fingers.

Yancey Clark looked with contempt
at the stricken Texan.

'Pity,' he said, 'that he won't have
time to heed those lessons he learned.'

Ruby unbuckled his gunbelt and
handed it back to its owner.

'I'll have my own gun back,' he told
Clark.

The gang-leader hesitated.

'We have a deal,' Ruby said, in a

no-nonsense tone of voice.

Yancey Clark hesitated a spell longer. Then, grinning, he went and fetched Ruby's gun from his saddle-bag. However, as he saddled his horse, Frank Ruby remained on his guard. He was expecting Clark to go back on his word — maybe even get a bullet in the back as he prepared to leave the camp. It came as a surprise when mounted up, that he rode out of the camp unimpeded, escorted by two of Clark's men.

'Tell Sarah I was asking for her, Frank,' Clark called after him. 'Might even pay a visit some day soon.'

Ruby drew rein and turned in his saddle to deliver a fiery ultimatum.

'You come near Sarah, Clark, and I'll kill you, so help me God.' Ruby's eyes swept the camp. 'And that goes for any other man jack of you too.'

'Now where's your good old Dixie hospitality, Frank?' Clark chuckled.

Yancey Clark had not exchanged a single word with the men accompanying Ruby. But it was well understood that at the first opportunity they would kill him. The outlaw leader would not risk Ruby changing his mind and riding to town, once the threat to his well-being had been lifted. But Ruby, knowing Clark's scurrilous nature, had not been fooled. He was only too aware that the men riding with him were, should he give them the chance, his executioners.

★   ★   ★

Jack Smithers' footsteps faltered. Had that been a gunshot he had heard? He waited. Listened. A minute before, the three men he had been tailing had entered the bank. Had the men argued among themselves? Or was there someone already lurking in the bank? Then he thought of Bowie Quail's skill with a knife. He always carried two knives. Three men. Two knives . . .

It would explain why there was only a single shot.

Smithers' thoughts came together in

a rush. Bowie Quail was heisting the bank himself. And so were the other men, whom he had mistakenly thought were its protectors.

'Double-crossing bastard!' Smithers swore.

Peeved, he sidled up to the bank's rear door and eased it open.

* * *

'There's a shorter trail,' one of the men, the rangier of the two, told Frank Ruby as he joined the main trail back to the farm. 'Prospector's trail,' he explained, as they switched to the rutted and overgrown route. 'Ain't been used in a long while. Hills ain't got no more gold in 'em.'

'Won't this take more time?' Ruby questioned, looking at the sky showing the first streaks of light. 'Won't you fellas be wanting to join up with the rest of the outfit to heist that bank?'

'Don't you worry none 'bout us, Ruby,' the second man, bulkier of stature than his partner, replied.

Ruby shrugged. 'All the same to me. Lead the way.'

The rangy man fell back, leaving Ruby vulnerable between him and his partner. The trail rose steadily into the hills until they reached a plateau from which the trail wound sharply downwards in a narrow track that ran along the rim of a canyon. Ruby reckoned that this was where Yancey Clark's henchmen planned on bringing about his demise.

A nudge would do it.

They could have shot him, of course. But gunfire in the morning stillness might start folk wondering, especially the kind of folk which the Clark gang would be anxious to avoid; folk like searching lawmen and the string of posses hunting them. Ruby had heard that following a recent train hold-up, the railroad had hired a posse with orders to keep looking until Yancey Clark and his riders were either dead or behind bars. And that posse was made up of former lawmen and bounty hunters, with a sprinkling of *hombres* who would slit their own mothers' throats for a nickel. Ruby guessed that with so much heat, a successful bank robbery to fund a stay in some other territory, probably south of the border or in an outlaw roost, was needed. And with gunplay there was always the risk of ending up on the wrong end of the affray.

Ruby drew rein on the plateau.

'Don't see the sense of coming this way, fellas,' he said. 'This trail is in such a poor state that snails are outpacing us.'

Neither of the men answered him, and offered no explanation or comment.

'I figure,' Ruby continued, 'that it would be sensible to backtrack and pick up the trail we left. A misplaced hoof or horses nudging could send a man plummeting into that canyon.'

Clark's hardcases exchanged quick glances, confirming their intentions.

'Thing is,' Ruby shook his head, 'no telling who that might be.'

Frank Ruby tensed when the rangy man shifted in his saddle, the way a man might to draw or grab a rifle.

The next couple of seconds would decide the next couple of decades.

★ ★ ★

Jack Smithers could hear voices.

'Two hundred thousand dollars.' Bowie Quail speaking. 'Just waiting behind that safe door, Billy Bob.'

'Bowie,' Hall said, shakily, 'I got a feeling that we should just walk away and forget this whole caper.'

'Not your darn moods again!' Quail snapped. 'Get out of my way. I'll open the damn safe.'

Smithers took advantage of the angry exchange to creep across the bank and hide under the teller's hatch directly facing the bank manager's office door. There was a lamp on the floor, its glow barely flickering. The man arguing the toss with Quail, Smithers recognized as the man with whom Quail had been in a heads-together conversation in the saloon the night before. He did not know the man, but having heard Quail address him as Billy Bob, Smithers reckoned that he was looking at none other than Billy Bob Hall, the West's master safecracker. It was said that the lock which Billy Bob Hall could not open, was a lock that had not yet been invented.

'Bowie . . . ' Billy Bob whined, pleadingly.

'I'm opening the damn safe, Billy Bob.' Quail shoved his partner aside. His pistol flashed in his hand. 'That's an end of it. And I don't give a shit how many bad feelings you've got!'

Billy Bob Hall stepped back. Bowie Quail was frustrated and angry enough to use the gun he was holding.

'I still can't figure out why the bank would leave so much loot in the safe unguarded,' Hall pondered.

'You worry too much,' Quail grunted,

and began to haul the heavy safe door open while holding the safecracker under threat of his .45.

Bowie Quail had an untrusting nature. He was a man who could not be trusted himself, so he saw no merit in other men's exhortations of trust and friendship. He had too often witnessed the falseness of such exhortations when the prize had been a whole lot less than the one he was about to reveal. He had seen throats cut for a dollar.

Jack Smithers' thoughts raced at a dizzy pace. Not the brightest wick in the West, it took time for his thoughts to gell. But of one thing he was sure, he wanted some if not all of what was in the bank safe. He would worry later about having Yancey Clark dogging his tail. Anyway, with a share of the riches in the bank safe he could start up his own outfit, the equal of Clark's.

The safe door swung open. There was a cranking noise from inside the safe which puzzled Bowie Quail. He grabbed the lamp and held it up to see what was making the sound, and froze.

* * *

Frank Ruby said, 'Cards on the table, fellas?'

'Don't know what you mean,' the rangy man said.

'Sure you do,' Ruby said. 'I know Yancey Clark better than the lines on the palm of my hand. And there was never any chance of him letting me ride free. I've been waiting for you boys to make your move. And I reckon that your plan was to make that move somewhere along that narrow trail we're headed into.'

The man exchanged glances with his partner. Frank Ruby's hand rested on his gun butt.

'Now like I said, I'm turning back,' he stated. 'So you fellas make up your mind if you want to settle this matter right now.'

The man said, 'That don't make no

sense, Ruby. Why would Hal and me risk goin' headlong into that gorge when we could have shot you a hundred times 'long the way?'

'You didn't shoot me, because you didn't want the sound of gunfire to be heard by ears which Yancey Clark and the entire outfit might not want to hear. Like the posse the railroad organized to hunt you down.

'As I hear it, they're being led by an Indian who could pick up the trail of a ghost. And I figure that Yancey Clark wants that bank loot badly to finance a long stay out of sight, with the hope that out of sight will also be out of mind.'

'Clever fella, ain't ya, Ruby?' the man called Hal said.

'When it comes to putting two and two together, I usually come up with four,' Ruby said.

Hal's partner said, 'If we let you be you'll ride for town. Then Yancey will peel the skin off our hides inch by inch.'

'You're small cogs — '

'We ain't that small,' Hal growled.

Ruby continued, 'Chances are that Clark will not reckon it worth his while to give chase . . . '

'You said you know Yancey,' Hal said. 'Seems to me that you don't know him very well. The man is meaner than a rattler, and a thousand times more deadly.'

'Think it through, fellas,' Ruby reasoned. 'If Clark successfully robs the Watts Ridge bank, he'll be heading south of the border, or seeking the refuge of a roost for a long time to come. Right now I reckon I can take you boys, so the choice is clear: risk getting killed now, or take your chances on Clark being too busy to even know you're gone.'

With Clark's honchos dithering, Ruby added, 'Anyway, the chances are that the railroad posse will close in on the outfit soon now. Territory to manouevre in is becoming smaller and smaller, isn't that so?'

'That's so,' Hal admitted.

'You fellas don't want to be around when that posse comes a-calling. Now do you?'

The rangy man said, 'I've been thinkin' 'bout that a whole lot of late, Hal.'

'It's been kinda on my mind too, Ben,' Hal said.

'Captured,' Ruby said, 'Clark and every man still standing will hang. Probably from a tree where they're found. I can't see the posse having any hankering to haul them back the long miles to the territorial capital, can you?'

The two men shook their heads.

'Right. No man with any sense would make that journey with a bunch of snakes in tow. You kill a snake where you find it or risk it biting you in the ass.'

'Ruby's making a whole lot of sense, Ben,' Hal said. 'I say we should hit the trail while we've still got the chance. We could head for some place like Canada. We ain't that well known anyway. Should be easy for you and me to kinda blend in. A year from now, no one would know us from Adam.'

Ben was still not wholly convinced.

'Better than dyin' like a dog, ain't it?' Hal pleaded.

Ben still tossing things in his mind, Hal became impatient.

'Well, I'm lightin' out anyways,' he said.

Hal urged his horse forward. Ben's hand dropped to his gun. Ruby tensed. He could not stand by and watch murder being done. Then Ben pulled his hand back.

'Hold up, Hal,' he called. He turned to Frank Ruby. 'Never afore came 'cross such a slick-talkin' cuss likes of you, Ruby. Good luck.'

'You too, fellas,' Ruby said.

The two men picked up their pace, anxious to put as much distance between them and Yancey Clark as quickly as possible.

Frank Ruby breathed a sigh of relief. His smile, when he could smile, was a wry one.

190

'Maybe,' he told himself, 'with talking ability like you've got, you should stand for political office.'

The mare snorted.

Ruby laughed. 'You figure so too, do you?'

The sky was lightening rapidly. Yancey Clark would be on the move soon. The detour on which his men had taken him added miles to his journey, and he would be hard pushed to reach town ahead of the Clark gang. And if there was time left to warn the town about Clark's arrival on their doorstep, then it would likely be only minutes.

For the briefest of moments, Frank Ruby thought about simply collecting Sarah and returning to the farm. He owed Watts Ridge nothing. But he soon realized that though Watts Ridge was a tiny part of the West, if he turned his back and minded his own business as most men would have, the happenings in town would feed the cancer of lawlessness and terror that had the folk of the West living in fear from minute to minute. There were more good men than bad men. And if good men stood shoulder to shoulder, the bad men could not prevail. The problem was, of course, the same as it had been throughout history: someone had to risk putting his head above the rim.

Grim-faced, Frank Ruby pointed the mare towards Watts Ridge.

19

'What's that darn handle on the side of the safe for?' Billy Bob Hall wondered aloud, his attention captured by the slam of the handle into a groove.

Bowie Quail's eyes popped as he saw the spring mechanism inside the bank safe click into place. A clamp held a six-gun in place directly in line with him. A mechanical claw, like a monstrous finger, was curled around the six-gun's trigger. For Bowie Quail, the grim discovery unfolded in slow-motion. Whereas in real time the whole procedure was lightning quick. The gun blasted, hurtling Quail back across the office. The thunder of the exploding gun shook the bank windows. The bullet which had ripped through Bowie Quail's chest and out through his back, tore a chunk of wood from the teller's hatch. It buzzed above Jack Smithers' head and ripped a hole in the crown of his hat. Unable to remain still, so sudden and violent had the incident been, he sprang up. For a confused moment, he and Billy Bob Hall stood looking at each other.

Conscious of how the town would react to the gunfire, Smithers vaulted over the counter and grabbed the fat sacks of bills from the safe.

'Stuff them inside your shirt!' he ordered Hall, and proceeded to do likewise with the remaining sacks.

Billy Bob Hall, unnerved by Quail's demise, and realizing how close he had come to being blasted into eternity, obeyed without quibble.

With the sounds of folk stirring, Smithers said, 'That's all we've got time to grab. It's most of it anyway.' He hauled a shocked and confused Billy Bob Hall along with him. 'Come on. Be a real shame to die, now that we're stinkin' rich!'

Smithers guided Hall through the town's backlots, emerging further along the street and directly opposite the livery. Men, most of them in night shirts, were running towards the bank bearing a wide variety of weaponry, most of which would likely explode in their faces when they tried to use the guns. But there were those, too, sporting the latest Colts, the kind of gun that had just blasted Bowie Quail to pieces.

Jack Smithers waited until the crowd's focus was on the bank. Then he sped across the street to the livery with Billy Bob in tow. The livery man, an oldster who was still rubbing the sleep from his watery eyes, smartly woke up when he was looking down the barrel of Smithers' pistol. He shoved the old-timer back inside and closed the livery gates. He clipped the livery man on the side of the head, sending him back to sleep.

He quickly saddled two of the best horses in the livery, figuring that horse-thieving was now a minor offence to bank robbery. Horses readied, he inched open the gates and peered out. The crowd milling around the bank were listening to a report about the happenings inside from two men who had come back out of the bank.

'Where the hell is the marshal, anyway?' an angry man wanted to know.

Mounted up, Jack Smithers and Billy Bob Hall, the latter still somewhat adrift of reality, ambled out of the livery. Observing the wild glint in Hall's eyes, Smithers held a firm grip on the safecracker's reins to prevent him from making a headlong gallop. He pointed.

'It ain't far to that bend. Once there, we can make fast tracks.'

'Any second now,' Hall worried, 'we'll be spotted and dead.'

'Just a short way now,' Smithers encouraged the safecracker.

Quiet as ghosts, Jack Smithers and Billy Bob Hall crept out of Watts Ridge.

★   ★   ★

Frank Ruby was on the edge of town when he heard gunfire. Not knowing what he was riding into, he eased back on his gallop. Yancey Clark might already be in town. His caution served him well. Seeing two riders sneak out of town, he left the trail and sought the shelter of a cluster of trees at the side of the road, where he waited until the riders, now picking up their pace, drew level with him. Toting a rifle he barred their passage.

Billy Bob Hall instantly reached for the sky. But Jack Smithers, determined to hold on to the bank loot, dived for his six-gun. Ruby shot him. When he tumbled out of the saddle his shirt burst open and the sacks full of dollar bills were strewn on the road.

Discarding his pistol and rifle, Billy Bob Hall hurriedly and breathlessly reassured Frank Ruby, 'You'll get no trouble from me, mister.'

Hall quickly unloaded the cloth sacks from inside his shirt.

Ruby collected the sacks and, unsure

of who was coming, he hurried back into the trees and hid the sacks of money in a hole in the trunk of a rotten tree. The crowd from outside the bank put in an appearance to hold him under threat of at least twenty guns.

'It's that stinkin' Reb again,' the large-bellied man Ruby knew as Charlie Koontz, who had tangled with him when he had ridden into town, growled. 'I said we should have hanged him then.'

He strode forward.

'Well, it's real nice of you to give us a second chance, Reb.'

Another man came running with news that only compounded Frank Ruby's plight.

'Marshal Ryan's been busted up somethin' awful.'

Koontz yelled, 'Someone get a rope to hang this Dixie bastard!'

There was no shortage of willing hands to haul Ruby to the hanging tree. In the confusion, Billy Bob became part of the milling crowd, but slowly drifted to the back of the crowd and finally out of it. There was that bank money waiting to be collected.

'Where's the bank's money?' the crowd badgered Ruby, as they hauled him steadily towards the hanging tree, a stout oak at the opposite end of Main.

They had already searched his saddle-bags.

'Hang me and you'll never find that money.'

This sobered some of the crowd. However, the fanatical Reb-haters, led by Koontz, were not going to be deprived of venting their spleen on a Southerner.

Koontz said, 'The money's some place close by. We'll find it.'

'I don't know, Charlie,' a man in the crowd doubted.

'We could be searching for a lifetime and not find it,' another man said.

'The Reb ain't never goin' to tell us where he hid the money,' Koontz argued. 'Why should he? As soon as he tells us we'll hang him anyway. Besides,' he growled, 'ain't you folk forgettin' that he murdered three citizens?'

'There's no proof of that,' the first man who had spoken out said.

'Proof!' Koontz chanted. 'He's a damn stinkin' Reb. That's proof enough for me.'

'Let's get this hanging over with, right now,' one of Koontz's sidekicks demanded.

'Hold it,' Ned Ryan's weak voice called out.

The marshal had come swaying from the law office toting a rifle that was more of a danger to himself than any threat to the lynch mob.

Koontz, dismissive of the marshal's intervention, ordered his cohorts, 'String him up.'

Ned Ryan attempted to intervene further but collapsed on the boardwalk.

Ruby was feeling the bite of the lynch rope on his neck when a shotgun boomed out, shattering the branch of the tree from which he was to swing.

'Cut him loose!' Jed Hanson ordered.

'Then back off.'

The man who had just tightened the noose round Ruby's neck undid his work, and cut the rope binding his wrists.

'Have you taken to likin' Rebs, Jed?' Koontz taunted Hanson. 'Have you forgotten what they did to your wife?'

Hanson said, 'I haven't forgotten, Charlie. But I've come to learn that all Rebs aren't bad. As all Yankees aren't good.'

Koontz and the hardcore of lynchers moved towards Hanson, but he remained steadfast.

'I'll use this blunderbuss' he threatened.

The men, knowing Jed Hanson as a man who never made idle threats, held back.

Ruby stepped forward.

'I can fight my own fights, Hanson,' he said gruffly.

'Suits me just fine, Reb,' Koontz growled.

They were squaring up to each other

when the same man who had come running with news of Ryan's injuries came running again, yelling, 'Riders coming.'

'How far off?' Ruby enquired urgently.

''Bout ten minutes' riding time, I figure.'

'That'll be the Yancey Clark gang,' Ruby explained.

'Yancey Clark!' was the horrified wail of the crowd.

'He's coming to rob the bank,' Frank Ruby informed them.

'Ain't nothing left to rob,' a man close to Ruby said.

'But Yancey Clark doesn't know that,' Ruby replied. 'I didn't rob the bank, but I have the bank's money stashed away safe and sound.'

Hanson stepped forward, his countenance forbidding.

'It was Clark and his curs who raped and killed my wife.'

Angered beyond reason, Hanson strode forward to meet Clark when he rode in. Ruby stepped in front of him.

'No point in throwing away your life, Hanson,' he said.

'I haven't got a life,' Hanson grated. 'Not since my woman was murdered. Now step aside.'

Frank Ruby stood firm.

'My plan,' he said, 'is for as few as possible of the Clark gang to ride out of this burg.' He turned to the crowd. 'We can take a stand for decency and right-living in this town, or we can crawl and hide and let Yancey Clark and his outfit terrorize us. The choice is yours.'

'You're takin' a stand against a Reb?' Koontz grunted.

'I'm taking a stand against a cur who has disgraced the name of good men, mister,' Ruby said. 'Now is there anyone else going to stand with me?'

'Count on me,' Jed Hanson said, grimly.

Ruby thanked Jed Hanson.

'But we'll need more than two men,' he said. 'If this town isn't to suffer the brunt of Yancey Clark's spite.'

The voice which finally urged the crowd to action was that of Charlie Koontz.

'The Reb's right. We've got to take a stand. What's your plan, Reb?'

'Simple,' Ruby said. 'A dozen men inside the bank as a reception committee. And a dozen more outside when Yancey Clark tries to flee the surprise in store for him. But right now the town must look like it's still sleeping.'

The crowd scattered, leaving behind only the men who had volunteered to back Frank Ruby. Not two dozen, as he had requested. Just six.

'Three inside. Three as outside back-up,' he said.

In the last couple of minutes, Ruby had noticed the absence of the second bank-robber he had apprehended, and figured that he knew where he had got to in the confusion. And he also knew that, should he not be able to produce the bank's money as he had promised, he would be right back at the end of a rope once, and if, Yancey Clark had been dealt with.

★　★　★

Conscious of every ticking second, Billy Bob Hall's search for the bank loot was frantic. But, finally, he had found it in a hole in a rotten tree trunk. He was hauling out the first sack when he heard a shuffle of feet behind him. He turned, alarmed, and was then terrified. He was certain that Jack Smithers was a ghost.

'You're dead!' Billy Bob whimpered.

'Cheatin' bastard,' Smithers croaked.

Blood foaming from his mouth, he swung the rock he had in his hand and smashed Billy Bob Hall's skull. His final smidgen of life spent, he fell to his knees, curled up and died.

★　★　★

The sound of hoofs was in the air when Ruby and his volunteers hurried inside the bank, locking the door as if the bank were closed. Hanson and his men took up positions in windows across the street from the bank, ready to spring a surprise at the appropriate moment.

Inside the bank, Frank Ruby ordered, 'Let them walk right in before you start shooting.'

They took up positions behind the teller's counter.

★　★　★

Yancey Clark's second-in-command was worried about Bowie Quail and Jack Smithers' whereabouts.

'Nothing to worry about, Scottie,' Clark reassured his right-hand man. 'Bowie and Smithers will be right there in town as a surprise package when we ride in.'

Scottie Blane was not as sure as Yancey Clark about that.

'Maybe we should temper our approach some, Yancey,' he suggested. 'Until we see what's in store.'

'In store?' the gang-leader scoffed,

and stated impatiently, 'What's in store is a town full of running chickens!'

Yancey Clark led the charge into Watts Ridge with even greater zeal. The gang galloped full out along Main, guns blasting.

'Scare them plenty,' was Yancey Clark's exhortation.

Store windows shattered, and the walls and boardwalks were peppered by a hail of venomous lead.

'Get up, you lazy Yankee bastards,' Clark yelled. 'Yancey Clark's back in town.'

He galloped on to the bank. Two men took charge of the horses while Clark led the gang inside the bank, kicking in the door with a swagger.

'Take that dynamite to the safe,' he instructed the gang's powder-man. 'And let's rob this damn bank, boys!'

Guns opened up from behind the teller's counter. Six men folded. The remaining outlaws turned tail, crowding the door. Three more joined the six. Yancey Clark, quick-witted as ever, crashed out through the window. Bloodied, he was still as dangerous as the wounded animal he was. More guns began blasting from the windows across the street. Bodies piled up. Clark grabbed one of his own men and used him as cover to reach his horse. The hapless outlaw took a dozen bullets, but he was an effective shield. Yancey Clark was in the saddle and swinging his horse to gallop out of town when, from the dust of the slaughter a grim-faced spectre, brandishing a Greener loomed up in front of him.

Jed Hanson's shotgun boomed. Yancey Clark, blasted out of his saddle, was reduced to a bloody ball of raw meat. The thunder of gunfire ceased and a ghostly stillness settled over the town of Watts Ridge. Jed Hanson threw away his weapon having no further use for it, now that he had wreaked his revenge on the man who had ruined and poisoned his life.

Frank Ruby came from the bank, saddened and sickened by the carnage.

He vaulted into his saddle, and turned his horse. He made his way to the place where he had hidden the bank's money and returned with it to the marshal's office, where he handed it over to Ned Ryan, looking perkier under the doc's care.

'Come visit soon, Marshal,' he said. 'Sarah would like that.'

He left the law office and regained his horse. Charlie Koontz blocked his path. He proffered his hand, which Ruby took to shake.

'Be seein' you soon, Reb,' Koontz chuckled.

Frank Ruby rode on. The war for him he reckoned was finally over.

THE END

We do hope that you have enjoyed reading this large print book.

Did you know that all of our titles are available for purchase?

We publish a wide range of high quality large print books including:
Romances, Mysteries, Classics
General Fiction
Non Fiction and Westerns

Special interest titles available in large print are:
The Little Oxford Dictionary
Music Book, Song Book
Hymn Book, Service Book

Also available from us courtesy of Oxford University Press:
Young Readers' Dictionary
(large print edition)
Young Readers' Thesaurus
(large print edition)

For further information or a free brochure, please contact us at:
Ulverscroft Large Print Books Ltd.,
The Green, Bradgate Road, Anstey,
Leicester, LE7 7FU, England.
Tel: (00 44) **0116 236 4325**
Fax: (00 44) **0116 234 0205**